DRAGON HO

By Amanda M

DEDICATION

To R, and to summer nights spent under the stars.
(DO NOT. FORGET. THE BUGSPRAY!)

Pssst. You. Yeah, you.

THE HEROINE'S NAME is Nalle. Hilarious readers have shared what it does to some of you when you don't know how to pronounce a name, so I thought I'd get you set up from go so that you're not popped out of the pages every time you see this five-letter wonder. *Nalle* is Finnish (and means *Teddy Bear,* and is sometimes a nickname given to people named *Björn,* which is *Bear* in Swedish). Nalle is pronounced *Nawl-ley.* (Want to hear it spoken? Listen to rock climber Nalle Hukkataival's friends shout encouragement in this clip: https://youtu.be/CQfPC4WZy4Q?t=128)

PROLOGUE

Nalle

IN ALL OF THE PLAINS on the great Isle of Venys, there are two types of theft that cause the greatest devastation among tribes: penis reft and cum raids.

If you're a Venysian inhabitant, you're well aware of the fact that the most valuable object in all of the land is a man of good breeding ability.

Because Venys needs men.

Why do females outnumber males to such a vast degree? Why the enormous disparity?

Legends and tales abound, but none of our people know for sure. My village, the North Plains Tribe, no longer cares to seek out the why of male scarcity. Instead, we concentrate on how best to keep us from extinction by protecting our males and using them as fairly as possible for repopulating the tribe. The few men left to us are equal to precious treasure, and that's true of males anywhere. Thus, the men-raiding.

The things women will do to secure a clutch with a man are detrimental to tribes. Penis reft, for example, is straight-up man theft, where a marauding tribe captures another tribe's menfolk and steals them for their own tribe's breeding purposes.

Cum raids would seem, on the surface, to be preferable to losing breeding men. A cum raid is where women sneak into camps and villages, slip into the breeding lodges, and gag a man so he can't call out for help. They ride the male, encouraging him with every asset they have available—be it their mouths or cock rings—to keep him in a swollen, semen-spewing, rigid state. They don't *steal* the male specimen; they only steal his cum, racing off at dawn with it dripping from between their thighs, leaving an exhausted, used man behind, sore and drained.

Give him a little time to recover and he'll easily be able to impregnate his tribeswomen again. He's not lost to the women of his village forever. But the danger in cum raids is insidious: if one of the raiders gives him the shaft chancre—or crotch crickets, or trichy itch, or any number of the riddling diseases, infections, and bugs that jump from rider to dick—he could go on to infect his whole tribe. Depending on the type of prick rot he contracts and what he passes to his women, it could cause everything from miscarriages to suffering babies. There are whole generations of tribes who've grown up with oddly swollen joints, impaired vision, sharp body pains, saber shins, and dental defects—all because they were fathered by a man who was genitally compromised on a cum raid.

The only ones spared will be the women too pregnant or too fresh from a delivery to have bothered riding him. And a tribe can't thrive with puny numbers of healthy people. And while things may be different in the jungles or deserts of the southern hemisphere, or in the frozen wilds of the far, far north, in our corner of the world, we began to seek methods of aggressively guarding our men.

That's how I ended up mated to a dragon.

CHAPTER 1

Nalle

"DRAGONS ARE SMALL," Yatanak assured me. His grizzled face, seasoned by many harsh-winded winters and scorching summer suns, creased with a confident smile. "No bigger than a partapa. But very fierce."

We *need* fierce. Our tribe (smaller than some, with a good number of the women being my half-sisters) could use *serious* fierce. An adult male partapa would perhaps be as tall as my knee—not their withers, but the top of their head. I eyed Yatanak dubiously. "And one dragon can protect our tribe? One lone dragon, knee-high?"

Yatanak nodded. "It was said that there is nothing in the worlds that fights more ferociously than a dragon when he's guarding those under his protection."

It was promising news, and that's what spurred me to action. I cling to this hope of the ultimate knee-high protector as I rotate my wrist, whipping my hook-on-a-string in a lasso as I pick my way higher up the mountain.

The hook is a wicked-looking bit of curved metal about the size of my thumb. That's from joint to nail. It's too big for fish, but Yatanak decreed it would hook a dragon. As the eldest among our people, his sage advice is sought out often and followed always. It's hard to catch time alone with him. He may be aged to something resembling conifer bark, but his summer turf house is never empty because our women miss male company—and he's it.

As the last unrelated male for a chunk of my tribesisters (every female of The Great Antelope Hunt generation and older can safely take him to bed; everyone younger must wait for a new man or risk too-close bedroll relations) his status as the only breeding male available is quickly becoming a problem. Two sunrises ago when I passed his sleeping ground to begin my journey, I saw Hupta leaving his turf house, her hair a wild mess, a grin stretched across her face. Hupta is from the Buffalo Hunt generation, just as I am. The rule of healthy breeding says that she shouldn't be visiting any man's lodge unless his generation matches ours—because otherwise she could be bedding her own father.

Thankfully though, Yatanak's every feature is thrown strongly in his offspring and Hupta looks nothing like him. Provided they aren't related, the only danger now is Yatanak falling dead on top of her, his heart stopped from too much excitement, just like old Pellmoh.

That's how we used to lose most of our men.

With so few born, they're kept busy until the day—or night—they keel over. Yatanak says it's a fine way to go. But in the last few seasons, the boys in our tribe haven't had the chance to grow old: they've been kidnapped. They may live to an old age and die in blissful excitement—but in the wrong tribe, it's more likely that they'll die with a shackle affixed to their ankle and never see the outside of a cum tent until the day their dead body is carted out to a pit or pyre.

We don't want our boys to suffer that fate. It's our custom to hand-select a tribe who treats their men well, one that lets them have the run of the village or camp and lets each man decide how many women he feels like servicing in a day or night.

No forced breedings. No being shut up and kept *only* for the purpose of procreational use.

A young man who finds himself chained to a stake in the floor of a cum tent may not complain too much about his lot of lusty fucking, not at first, but at some point, he's going to grow to hate his tether. He's going to resent his captivity. And when he gets to be too difficult to handle, the women he's slaved to service—the mothers who forced him to sire their many children—are going to club him to death and replace him with a younger, more easily manageable male.

Sharply, I shake my head, trying not to think about it. Jöran, a boy birthed of my mother, was taken a quarter lunation ago.

'I'm not a boy anymore, Nalle. I'm a man,' he'd growl if he could have heard my thought just now.

We look nothing alike, we *are* nothing alike (different tribe fathers, we're certain), but we were close.

He came of age this summer. My brother was set to be traded to the Middle Plains' Tribe in exchange for one of their conscientiously-raised young men. The tribe of the Middle Plains lets their boys be boys just like we do. Lets them run and play with their sisters and they know their mother and their many aunts and they are free and happy. When they become men, the only thing to change in their existence is how they spend a good portion of their time.

A trembling smile tries to shine on my face when I think of Jöran's oft-made complaint that one day, he wouldn't have to do any weaving or washing. No more women's work for him when he came of age. He'd just lie on his back and make the *women* do all the work.

(For this statement, he'd often receive a good-natured cuff upside his blonde head.)

Now I'm afraid he's not laughing. I'm scared that wherever he is, he's probably strapped down on his back and isn't enjoying all the work happening on top of him like he was sure he would. That it's not all 'lazing about and relaxing' like he joked it would be.

Because it was the Qippik tribe who abducted him. The Qippik Tribe's cruel, raiding claws have a way of sinking into young men and leaving them hollowed husks they don't bother to burn or bury. We came upon their men once. They'd left them dead on the plains for the scavengers, these ill-used fathers of their children, these human beings who deserved a full life even if their purpose was merely to seed every eligible woman who visited them.

I whip my hook-on-a-string at a sapling, catching a leaf and angrily winding it back to me.

We aren't strong enough to rescue Jöran from the Qippiks.

Yet.

But once we have a trained dragon at our feet, perhaps we'll stand a chance. In fact—

Burnt.

I tilt my head, catching the scent on the wind.

Banked fire. Yatanak told me to follow the *banked fire.*

I didn't know what he meant. Half the time, I suspect he talks in riddles to sound wise but cover the fact he's forgotten the answer to anyone's question.

I suck in a breath, lungs punching my ribs as I smell *burnt* that should not be here; there are no other tribes on this mountain, not this high up.

I'm watching for a burrow, or a wee den.

I don't expect a cave.

It's ginormous.

My feet trip as I near the entrance. The rocks are craggy, and I'm bound to break my damn neck if I don't keep my eyes on my feet. But I'm trying to scan the area, on the lookout for a scaly little creature to scuttle past me on its way to hide.

I compromise by moving slowly, glancing at the ground to pick the next safest step, then peering around for the shy, rare creature.

I can't wait to start training it. Yatanak said dragons are loyal to the one who captures them. Lord knows we could use a loyal, protective creature.

Without it, we're stuck being nearly helpless.

I grit my teeth.

Not for long.
I'm going to catch a protector.
I'm going to win us a dragon.

CHAPTER 2

Nalle

I WAS NOT PREPARED for traveling in darkness. This far from the cave entrance, I can barely see. I wonder if I should risk bringing out my candle, lighting the wick. Without a doubt, it will alert my quarry. Dragons are supposed to be very observant and react with the swiftness of a grass snake's escape.

Once trained, it's possible that they can strike with all the swiftness of a stealthy grass snake too. I silently send up a prayer that this is true. Harnessed, this will be *exactly* what we need: a small but fierce companion to shadow us. Like a trained wolf, but with scales.

The scrape of rock-on-rock makes my ears perk.

Excitement hits my chest like a tentpole hammer. *Please be a dragon.* Heart racing, I fix my eyes on the corner I think I heard the sound come from. All I see is endless black.

No, wait... I squint. There's a little shine—

I hear a scrape, and at first, I think I'm seeing a gigantic, inky-dark snake-like creature. That's bad enough. A rock python is a dangerous beast. But as my eyes follow the length of the thing, and triangular wedges become apparent as the thing curves up, up, up—I see the shapes are actually erupting out of the sinewy form like a crocodile.

I'm staring at a creature's *tail*.

A soft glow turns on above my head, illuminating my field of vision.

My racing heart?

Stops *dead*.

Fear pours down my spine like icy lake water. I'm staring at a massive haunch. Scales, that's what shined and caught my eye. Glimmery black scales.

Dragons have scales.

I'm staring at a dragon's *butt*.

And immediately I know that Yatanak's information was a little off. Dragons might be knee-high—but only when they're fecking *babies*.

I'm afraid to breathe. Afraid to move. I'm afraid to close my eyes. I stare at the dragon's ass and try to discern if I can feel my feet. Because I'm going to need to run faster than the creature can wheel around and bite.

Or blow fire. *Yatanak sent me off with some size assurances—lies!—and a* fishhook? *The old man is bat-guano CRAZY!*

The glow coming from above me shifts.

Sucking in a silent, terrified hiccup, I crane my head back and cast my gaze high, high up.

Two giant eyes shine down on me, turning everything a glowing green.

Leathery whispers signal that wings are being adjusted behind the great creature, unseen for all the black. Unseen even with the green glow because it's me who has all the dragon's formidable focus.

A curdled scream dies in my throat.

The dragon's head is long with a wedge-scythe hook on the end of its snout. Its upper jaw juts out with fangs, and its teeth poke out and overlap its lips on the lower side. Behind its head are two horns, and if I'm not mistaken, the slight ruff at its throat is actually a relaxed frill.

I'm staring up at a Great Crested Merlin. A dragon of legend that none of my people have ever seen—or at least never returned home to confirm that the tales are true.

Tribes from the Steppes have all the dragon stories, claims so outlandish that no one believes them. *Tall as a mountain,* they've said. *Swifter of wing than an eagle. Firebreath so hot it can melt a woman in full armor where she stands.*

Dressed in nothing but animal skin and flammable fur, I gulp.

Two triangular scales situated superior to the nostrils of the creature flare up like nasal shields. They twitch back as the dragon inhales, the creature taking breath in hard even as it parts its jaws. *The dragon is scenting me.* Its eyes, the color of early prairie grass stems, narrow.

Pupils that sit like black slits in jewel-like eyes focus on me and flare wider—and goosebumps break out along my skin.

"I'm sorry to disturb you," I wheeze through a choked throat. "I'm going to go—"

The snout of the beast comes crashing down, its maw open wide.

Without thought, my hands act.

I whip my hook.

My tiny, ineffectual hook.

Hot steam sprays me—and the dragon's jaws wrench in opposite directions as it twists its head and snorts, torquing its neck as it peers down its long nose to determine what I've tossed.

My tiny little hook's string snaps free without so much as a fight. And why would it? A spider's web has more tensile strength than the tiny cord. I wasn't intending to reel in a sky monster.

Caverock shakes down from the ceiling as the dragon looses a growl so low in frequency that I can't even hear it—I can only *feel* it.

The beast's claws flex, scraping the rocky ground with painful screeches that have me ducking. With dread, I wince and peer up, trying to see what I've hooked.

The beast's nose.

I have this monster caught by its *nose.*

The massive dragon has gone still, its frightfully intelligent eyes briefly crossing as it inspects the shiny metal stabbing right through its thin-scaled nasal shield.

Slowly, the beast's focus straightens, and its incensed gaze trains on me.

I'm going to die.

CHAPTER 3

HALKI

I WILL KEEP HER FOREVER.

My nostrils flare again, the bite of pain from her strange extending claw stuck in my flesh barely distracting me as her scent wafts into my nostrils anew.

I know this scent. I KNOW this female.

She takes one measured step backwards. Her other heel lifts up as if she plans to keep retreating.

Oh no, drhema. You won't be leaving. I clap my hands around her.

She shrieks like a baby deer and struggles between my palms like a mouse.

Mmm. I haven't bothered to hunt mice since I was a hatchling. The oblong scales of my upper lip pull tight as my mouth crooks up in a smile. I sort of miss their taste. Their little kicks as my throat muscles squeezed them down.

Just thinking about eating one makes me hungry.

But first, I will see to my newest treasure. I still can't believe she *clawed* me.

"Knee-high!"

The words explode from between my hands, causing my neck frill to flare wide before slapping back against my throat again.

I drop onto my haunches and lower myself down on my elbows. Then I open my hands to get a better look at her.

If she were a mouse, I'd be eating her.

But I know her—there's no way I could forget her. Her very presence here, in my cave where she's travelled so far to seek me out, it's making my heart speed up. So no, I won't be eating this creature of mine. Even if her furry-humped back looks more animal and less human and so completely different from when I last saw her. Actually, nearly all of her looks different.

Two fear-wide eyes stare up at me. A keen terra cotta color, her irises are. These eyes, I could never forget. As unique as her scent and as equally exciting to my senses.

The hair on her head I remember well, but it does not match the hair that's grown on her hump. The hump is new. It must have sprouted when she reached adulthood. And her hump of hair doesn't match the tufts of fur that circles each of her wrists. She has yet another patch of fur sprouting up on her hind legs, with the long hair shafts thickly puffed out everywhere they wrap each hind foot.

I sniff, trying to scent her, and receive a sting for my effort. *Her damned claw.* I bend my neck forward, draw one hand from around her slight body, and pluck the claw out of my nose.

Ungh, that smarts!

With an irritated hiss, I hold up her silver claw and glower down at where I'm keeping my little prize cupped in my other hand.

"You would do well not to scratch at me with this again," I snarl.

It wasn't my intention for the words to sound so full of aggression, but it's difficult to articulate softness when you speak through fangs.

Rather than pledge her oath that she won't raise her talon to my face, rather than even providing an apology—she whirls and races right off my hand on her pair of shaggy hind legs.

Tossing her claw aside, I easily recapture her. My tail twitches lazily behind me as I ignore her screech and scoop her up to bring her to my eye level.

I open my jaws to suck her scent onto my tongue, permeating my senses with her even further.

Instantly, my blood speeds. *It's been moonscapes since I've smelled you. Stalked you.*

We were both adolescents then. I was much smaller, and she was much less hairy.

My eyes catch on the way she shivers, because the ring of fur humped up around her shoulders doesn't shudder with her.

Waxing crescents, you've turned out so strange.

Long ago, I was ordered to stay away from her. But she's stumbled into my cave and attacked me and I caught her so she's mine now. I don't care what she looks like. This female should have been in my keeping since we were children, and would have, if it wasn't forbidden to touch a human. I was punished harshly for getting as close to this one as I did.

And yet... I'm holding her in my hands, and all the dire warnings that ring in every hatchling's ears... none of the warnings have come true with her.

If I'm honest with myself, I'm experiencing a small degree of disappointment.

But this is fine. I can still keep her. I press my nose along her body, sucking in her scent, and immediately I'm entertained by an outraged squeal. When I rasp a laugh and puff at her, a rush of smoke travels under her skin, causing it to billow up before she slaps it back down.

Interesting.

Has she grown a frill, like my dragonkind have? A Crested Merlin like myself fans their frill for a variety of reasons: to express themselves, to accompany a mating dance, and to appear more formidable during a battle to protect your territory or your nest or your mate.

I puff again, watching her skin billow once more before she savagely slaps it down again.

"I want to see it," I tell her, and frown when she cowers on my hand.

Perhaps she's afraid to raise her frill to me. At her size and disadvantage when faced off with me, I can almost see why the average creature would hesitate.

But I have seen this female defend a lamb from slinking yotes using nothing more than a handful of rocks and her fearless stance and shouts. I would have thought she'd be fanning her frill at me like a hatchling faces off against a raiding wyvern. When cornered, a scrappy individual turns fierce.

And my still-stinging nostril says my human is scrappy.

Why did she come here?

I repeat the puff of air a third time, and when the top half of her skin bulges up from the force of my breath, I catch her frillskin with my teeth and tug.

She makes an outraged bellow as I peel up the loose flap. I don't pull hard; I don't want to injure her—I only want to see what her frill looks like. And she isn't making sounds of pain, just indignation.

Only, instead of the frill lifting up a little bit, it comes completely *off*—and her arms drop out.

I stare at what's revealed.

She doesn't have a hairy humped frillskin at all.

It was a covering.

Save for her fluffed legs and her furred wrists, she looks more than ever like the human girl I stealthily pursued.

And with her skin flap removed, her scent is even stronger.

My tail curls around us and I knit my talons behind her back, pulling her closer, almost as if I'm cradling her to my chest.

As I draw her to me though, she begins to fight, her limbs flying with the incoordination of a panicked meal. Hunger begins to war with curiosity. Then her flailing hand bangs me in my clawed nostril.

I snarl.

She freezes.

My chest rises with my inhale, and her sweet scent is so good, I unconsciously flick my tongue at the air, tasting her with my receptors.

She shudders against my chest scales, and I tighten my hands around her, squeezing her to me, loving the way she feels against the scales of my palms.

I've never touched a human before. Save for this one when we were both young, I've never been interested in trying. All the dragons in our mountain range are to avoid these little beasts, these pests. And we do. Herds of humans inhabit the plains, but my kind rarely even fly over them, let alone eat them, for fear that they'll matebond us by accident. We're instructed as fledglings that if we ever consume a human, then we are to crisp them thoroughly with our flames before touching them. Elder dragons are insistent about this, about the danger humans pose to us. And with the red moon touching the world within a lunation or less, this human should be especially dangerous to me.

The red moon is a phenomenon over the land of Venys, and it comes to visit every hundred years. For dragons, this means we'll undergo a month's worth of unrelenting mating fever.

I shift, my groin scales uncomfortably heated. I've been suffering the first discomforts of mating fever, and the blood moon has yet to burn in the sky. I took to my cave during the earliest pangs, irritable beyond reason. This will be my first blood moon heat, and I've been lust-fogged and struggling to come to terms with the inevitability that I've reached the end of my solitary days. Because the urge to mate feels like it will kill me if I don't give in, and once a Crested Merlin mates, he mates for life.

But I prefer to be alone.

Or rather, I've never met a dragon that I found compelling enough to bind myself to for the rest of my days. For my kind, our lives last centuries.

...Which is part of the reason we're warned away from humans. As a fledgling, I grew up on stories of dragons who were misfortunate enough to let a human touch them. When the human made contact, the dragons changed to human forms too and were trapped to live the same unbelievably short existence of their mate.

My brow scales bunch as I frown. Perhaps we've all been lied to. Perhaps the Elders are wrong. After all, who among them has ever bonded to a human? None. And now I hold this human in my hands—she *clawed* me, for skydrakes' sake—and I've not bonded to her.

I place a clawtip under her chin with care. When she refuses to raise her head for me, I smirk and add a little pressure until she hisses and her nose goes up, showing me her face, her flashing firespice eyes.

The renewed bolt of recognition makes my neck muscles weak. My snout sinks to the level of hers, and I stare into her captivating gaze closer than I've ever dared to before. Until I was caught and punished, I stalked this human.

I've missed her.

Of course the relief of being reunited is a little one-sided on account of her never seeming to realize I was behind her. Staring at her. Flickering up her scent and following her. Eating the rabbits she released for me.

(The North Plains' people don't eat rabbits, we're told. So she was likely emptying traps that caught the wrong type of quarry, simply not knowing I was right there, surprised as ever that she was feeding me.)

They were delicious.

She was probably no older than I was—my human, not the rabbit meals—and I wondered if she had snuck away from her herd to explore just as I had escaped the watchful eyes of my nestmasters.

Nestmasters are Elder dragons who tolerate hatchlings enough to become their teachers. My chief nestmaster taught all my nestmates, a whole passel of us, and because this dragon was older than God's moss, I was able to sneak away more often than I had to stay and mind him.

And sneak away I did. I roamed the plains pretending I was a black lion with a frilled crest rather than a shaggy mane. I caught mice, chased buffalo—and then got chased by buffalo because I was smaller than I thought I was and my fires weren't answering to my call yet.

It was a great time.

I would never have discovered this human if I hadn't heard her laughing. The grasses on the plains grow so tall in the summer that a human can almost walk hidden. A child certainly can. And this one was hidden from the sky, but I heard her bubbling laugh, and I swooped down to investigate.

She seemed to be skipping and singing and entertaining herself. Situated with my throat against the ground, I tried to pretend I was nothing but a dark bolder, and I watched her until the sun was nearly down. When she began her journey home, I followed her as far as I thought I could without being captured by her tribe. And the next day and the next, I found her playing in the grasses again by her lonesome, and with a predator's ability to hide in plain sight, I watched her again and again.

I only stopped when I was forced to. My drakon and drakaina (my sire and dam) were horrified to learn how close I came to a human.

"Isn't it strange that you would find me all these suns and moons later?" I murmur aloud. "I was sure you never knew I was there. Why *have* you sought my company?"

Eyes the color of sun-warmed rock meet mine and flick to my mouth. To where my teeth points aren't covered by my lip scales.

I cock my head. "Why do I have the sense that you can't follow a single word I say?"

Her gaze flashes to mine again, and then she's back to watching my mouth. Her chest is rising and falling, and I focus on the way her nose, framed by two small, nearly see-through membranes, flares. I've heard that humans have the worst senses—of smell and of sight and hearing, too. I wonder if that's true of this human.

Her eyes dart to the side. In the space of a moment, I get the sense she's preparing to escape me. She tenses—her intent very plain, although it seems she isn't aware of that.

You must eat a lot of green things. You'd make a terrible hunter.

When she ducks my thumb claw and tries to run, I'm ready. I simply clap my folded hands over her, squishing her to the cave floor.

She screeches and I feel pressure on my thumb.

Is she trying to *bite* me?

Ha! This is exactly like my mouse-hunting days. The same effectiveness for this mouse too.

Amused, I sweep my hands towards myself, making her whole body slide across the cave's stone floor. She hollers and shoves at my top hand, even kicking me, I think. Once she's tucked to my chest again, I carefully raise my hands and curl my neck back so that I can peer down at her.

She opens her jaws to spit out the mouthful of my digit like I taste bad to her.

How bizarre, because I'm almost certain she wouldn't taste bad to me.

She throws out her arm to slap at me.

Her hand lands right over my heart.

Lightning arcs between us.

The blinding flash is an arrow of pain. I bellow in shock.

Fire burns through my body—and dimly, I hear her yell too.

This I don't like at all. My tail lashes the air. It's a phantom stab to my heart, a further shredding of my already malfunctioning system to hear her pain, but I'm unable to do anything to help.

With spasms racking me, I try to draw my hands and claws against myself and far away from her, keeping her safe from the danger I pose, hopefully. My wings slap out and crumple, the thinly-scaled skin catching on the rough rock of the cave walls, my wing talons digging in as if they want to help fly me out of this pain. My long body tries to curl in on itself, and I collapse on my side, blinded and deafened and feeling all of my bones aching.

What is happening to me?

She touched my heart. A *human* touched right over my heart.

My femurs feel like they're being compressed. Each and every one of my bones begins to feel a similar squeeze. And I know without a doubt what's happening.

I'm turning into one of her kind.

CHAPTER 4

HALKI

EVEN AS MY BODY CONTORTS into something so many times smaller than is natural, I'm almost frantic, wondering if my female—my mate, the female who enchants my eye, my *drhema*—is still here. If she's waiting for me to finish my change into the form that will complement hers.

Through eyes slitted with pain, I try to raise my neck—and my head lifts with barely any effort expended because my long, heavy neck is no more. My skull is damn near attached directly to my shoulders.

Fried satyrs, it feels odd.

But my female is at my side. She waited for me.

She's trying to back away, but I have her shackled in place by my tail. Thank all that glitters that she couldn't leave—and that my tail hasn't disappeared yet. Maybe it won't.

It starts to shrink before my very eyes.

Basilisk's balls! "Damn it, *no*..." I try to say. Out of rubbery lips, my short tongue and flat teeth garble, "Dnggg! RRRGH!"

I swallow, and a bone slaps up and down along the thin skin inside the front of my throat. The area feels very... naked. There's no neck frill hugging just behind my jaws and halfway down my neck. I raise my hands up to my face, and find I still have claws. But they belong to a mountain cat's half-grown kitten, not a dragon.

I plant them on the cave floor and try to stand.

My hind legs are all krevk'd up. They drag behind me like dead weights until I gain my kneecaps. A fever-hot weight swings heavily between my legs and just behind it tugs something that feels like a giant pendulum, both of them seeming unnaturally tight for their skin and making my narrow human's pelvic region rage. With a confused contortion, I find the source: an overripe cock juts from my scale-less groin, and behind it, a swollen sac appears as if it's about to explode.

I can only stare. Because Crested Ancestors above—my innards are fully exposed, with no groin scales for them to tuck into!

Out of my throat comes a rasping, "Krevvvkehd!"

Huh. My human throat makes a near perfect approximation of curse words. Fancy that.

Gritting my teeth, walking on my hands and kneecaps, hauling the rest of my legs behind me along with my heavy tailbone, I try to reach my mate before my tail shrinks completely and she can make her escape.

With pain-bleary eyes, I look to her face and find her own eyes are wide. Her mouth is open and she's staring at me like I'm not her transformed dreams come true—but a *monster.*

"We have bonded," I try to say. "That spark that lit when you touched my heart? We are mates." What growls up from my throat doesn't quite convey what I hoped. It sounds like, "WeeARRGH'td!"

She shrinks back. And fair enough. She's unnerved at my inability to speak without growling at her.

I only need to practice, and I'll secure the ability. I'm a Crested Merlin. We're esteemed among all dragons, excelling at everything save for, perhaps, humility.

My long tail, which has been rapidly reducing, drops right off of her waist and shrivels into nothing. My tailbone feels instantly lighter—and it's a good thing because the loss of its weight means my lunge forward carries me as far as I hoped to reach.

My mate has whirled around, and she's going to race for the cave-mouth, I'm certain of it—

But she doesn't make it. Because I land on her.

CHAPTER 5

Nalle

IT FEELS LIKE A WHOLE bogdamn dragon comes crashing down on me.

That's because a whole bogdamn dragon *does* come crashing down on me. He just happens to be mostly man-shaped.

"UFFF!" My cheek smushes into the stone floor, and I absolutely cannot move under the male's great weight.

And he is a male.

As in, he's got the biggest tallywhacker I have ever seen.

My eyes pop open wide when he growls, his hands grip my waist—and something that feels thick as a broomhandle prods at my leather-covered ass.

"Get *off* me!" I holler.

I twist like a rabid weasel, fighting and shoving and cursing him until I'm splayed sideways and he's no longer poking at a danger zone with that weapon he's wielding.

My efforts though, have turned me so that I can see his face, and this view is no better than the cave floor. It's scarier, in fact.

He's a *dragon*man. Black wedge-shaped scales cover every inch of his skin, even tiny little ones that fit in the creases on either side of his eyes. These scales are the only small things about him. He's *huge* all over, his jaw hewn square, with hollows on either sides of his mouth that form carved depressions until the rounds of his cheekbones take over; the perfect masculine framing for his strong face. Dangerous brows sweep down from his forehead, and below them, his eyes are all dragon, with slits for pupils and irises that throw brightness like emerald lanterns. He's staring down at me like he's starving. *He's a dragon that turned into a man!*

How? And how do I get away from him?!

Hands big enough to span the length of my rib cage crush me in their grip. After a moment of staring at each other, the dragon sits back on his heels and tries to turn me over on my back.

...With the goal of assuaging his screaming erection, I can only assume.

But that's a no.

Because while I would have told any of my tribeswomen that I'd welcome the first unrelated male I've ever seen up close, I always envisioned taking a fully *human* man. With a normal, natural, human-sized rod.

This? The dragon's carrying a third leg with a mushroom cap, not a prick.

And that's not all. His, ah, 'member' is ridged, with raised bumps along the sides. Bumps that are seeping a slick amethyst fluid. From his tip, two feathery protrusions, not unlike moth antennae, emerge.

OH, NOT ON HIS LIFE!

Not for *anyone's* life! If you told me that a baby unicorn would die if I don't spread for this, I'd ask you where you want the foal buried! Just *NO.*

I fight him, resisting with bared teeth and breathless curses, bringing my arm up between us, trying to shove at his stone-like chest, his rock-hard arm.

He's not expecting me to nail him with a panicked punch to his upper right ribcage.

Livershot.

He drops over me with a gasping grunt. His hands have gone momentarily slack, no longer gripping me.

Which doesn't help me in my escape like I hoped it would. He must weigh a full wool bale, easy, and his weight is plopped smack on me so that I feel like I'm trying to crawl out from under exactly that much. "Get OFF! Get away from me!"

It's pretty unthinkable that I've uttered this. Here is a man I can have sex with. There are women who would *steal* this opportunity—literally. (Freakish reproductive equipment or not.) But all I want to do is run.

I'm inhaling to scream when his arresting face is suddenly shoved in mine. "Yeww ARRR," he growls. "Myyy *mrrrr.*"

Whatever declaration he's made seems to please him. He stares down at me with steadily lowering lids as his throat vibrates in a very *not human* purr.

Mouth hanging open, staring up at him, pinned with his heavy horse's cock slapping my upper thigh every time he exhales, I'm overwhelmed.

I just wanted to save my brother!

And then his hand cups between my legs, and his thumb tries to run along the crotch seam of my leathers.

I jump and struggle and hurl imprecations—at him, his cave, his damned winged-lizard mother—and try to beat him with my elbow.

For that maneuver, the dragon catches my elbow with all the ease he'd have shown if he caught the wing of a domesticated chicken. He brings my limb down until it rests on the cave floor.

"This isn't better," I mumble, eyes pinned by his.

He keeps his hand cupped over the crook of my arm, keeps me beneath him, and when I finally meet the dragon's eyes again, he eases himself up, reaches down, and catches me by my thigh.

I snarl with the effort I expend trying to thrash my way out from under him.

I have no luck with this though. He snaps up my knee so that my thighs are spread. He rolls my bottom half so that I'm twisted at the waist—and with a surprisingly skillful hand, he's exploring my antelope-hide leathers like he's searching for a key in the dark. I tanned the buck that made my clothes; I tanned him until his skin was hairless and butter-soft. Then the natural friction of my inner thighs worked the leather even softer when I walked. Now it's so supple, I don't know what the dragon feels, but I feel *him* when his curious finger brushes over my clit.

I squeak.

The dragonman's eyes flash neon. His finger presses over my clit with intention, where he rubs, testing.

I suck in a breath, bite my lips, plant my heels, and try not to squirm into his too-effective touch as I inch away from him.

He takes his hand from my elbow, grabs me by the hip, and drags me until I'm right where he wants me—back under him.

And then with a softer touch, he brings his finger back to the magic spot he's found, and he dances over it with a butterfly's pressure.

Through a layer of animal skin, it shouldn't be anything.

My body decides otherwise. It falls still. My commands sent to it are rendered completely ineffectual.

My thoughts even stutter. My *'Run away!'* turns into *'Ohhh... We'll run in just a moment...'*

Another silken touch has my breath catching in my chest.

Yet another gentle brush has me staring up at his face, at the intense look in his eyes as he scrutinizes my expression, and his questing finger has all the rest of my focus.

I twitch when he adds a second finger, petting over me. The leather was already warm from being against me—and with his touches, it's grown hot. It feels like it's melting me, turning everything below my belly to liquid.

I shift under him and exhale in a rush as he feathers his thumb lower, along the area that covers my slit.

His eyes, scrutinizing my face, flare before his expression sharpens, even as his lids lower and he repeats the sensual pass.

Instead of bracing to run, my legs tense to—to wrap around him.

Before I can give into the impulse to embrace his hips, the dragon's lips part—firm lips, the bottom one thicker, formed in a way that my eyes have trouble tearing away from it—and he sucks in a breath.

His nostrils flare and his eyes lock back on mine.

A sizzle of awareness explodes down my spine. It feels like my lower half lights up from this intangible contact.

And the dragon's gaze drops between my legs like he can tell. His hands move to my leather's waist fastening and he jerks on it, causing my butt to leave the ground for a brief moment before slapping back down.

Reality crashes into me. And I realize that no matter how much my body is interested in a male's skillful touch, my head is overwhelmed by this dragon. Panic fills my chest, making my body feel bisected; my turned-on lower half may be submitting to the dragon, but my rational head is floating above the scene, alarmed.

With no premeditation whatsoever, when my hands splay on either side of me, and my fingers brush against the metal hook that started all this trouble...

My hand closes over it.

My arm arcs up, crossing in front of me. I swing wide—only *nearly* catching him in the face, when I could have aimed the hook right for his eye.

With a guttural exclamation of shock, he falls back.

I scramble away. I don't even know how my legs manage it; everything felt like soaked weaving reeds a moment ago. Now adrenaline courses through my veins, and I pump my arms and my feet are swift and I fly out of the cave like I have wings.

A furious roar blasts out, rippling against me, making my back muscles snap tense.

But I don't stop running.

CHAPTER 6

Nalle

I'VE ANGERED THE BEAST. Enraged him, in fact.

And he's a man no more. From my hiding place, I watch the great black dragon (who appears even *bigger* and more menacing in what's left of the sun's light) as he tears up the ground, bellowing—and I watch as he grabs a tree. A full-grown, fifty-woman-tall tree.

He hurls it off the mountain.

The sound as it crashes against summit rock and other trees on its way down seems to bode ill. My odds of surviving the same fate?

I gulp.

I'm crouched, eyeing him from a thicket. I hope he doesn't get close because he's sure to smell my blood. I'm bleeding because my hiding place is a berry thicket, and when I ran into the evil-thorned berry canes, they tried to tear off all my skin. If I live through this, then the price of their camouflage was worth it. They have many, many chartreuse leaves providing me cover.

Glumly, I consider that if I still had my buffalo hide coat, I wouldn't be all torn up now. But it is what it is. On the plus side, I've been picking the canes clean and enjoying the berry-recompense at least. The berries are mildly sweet and full of juice. If their thorns hadn't dug trenches in my skin that sting like the dickens, I'd consider it a fair trade.

My plan is to get back down the mountain. My problem—besides the angry dragon—is that the longer I wait, the nearer to dusk the sky turns. In fact, it's quickly becoming dark.

The moon is visible; just a rim of colored light, looking spooky and so close it's like it's been hung just off the side of the mountain. It's almost scarlet tonight, and it's beautiful.

The sight of the black dragon against the darkening sky set with a nearly blood-red moon feels ominous enough. Add his temper tantrum and I'm not keen on moving out of my hiding place. *I'll just stay here, wait him out.*

The dragon drops his snout to the ground and inhales, his ribs showing briefly along his scaly sides. His wings snap up high above his withers and his tail falls still. With slow deliberation, he cranes his head in my direction.

Caught.

His long neck is a deadly curve of scales and spikes, with a bright-streaked neck frill that loosens and billows up like a sail on either side of his face.

I don't think twice: I peel out from the thicket, grimacing and gasping like a panicked animal as I get torn up on the berry canes a second time.

The dragon looses a loud roar at my retreat.

Scrambling, I trip and skid across the rocky ground. *"Ah!"* I yelp breathlessly, barely catching my footing enough to control my fall. I crack my knees on the rocks, and that's good, because rather my knees than my face, right?

Still. Ow.

The dragon growls furiously behind me, but oddly sounds no closer.

Risking a hurried glance over my shoulder, I find him standing still, which makes no sense, and stranger still, his muscles heave, flexing and twitching, like he wants to leap for me but he's holding himself back.

His eyes aren't green anymore. They're a solid, threatening obsidian that somehow still glows.

I don't know why he's restraining himself, but there's no way I'm wasting the opportunity to escape. With a gusty, sawing sigh of relief, I shove to my feet—and run.

Mistake.

I know better than to run from a predator. Really, I do.

With a roar that shakes the ground, the dragon tears after me again but I scamper for the rugged trail that will take me down the mountain. It's such a narrow pass that I nearly have to turn sideways to navigate it; there's no way it will permit the dragon's breadth.

He realizes the same.

And his bellow of enraged defeat will haunt my nightmares.

The screech of his claws raking across mountain rock is horrific as he vents his frustration, and I race away from him like my life depends on it.

YEP. RUNNING THROUGH the dark is stupid. I don't keep a wary eye on the sky. I don't even look back. It took me almost a day and a half to make the trek up the mountain, but racing down in the dark like a terrified deer, I skid and fall and tumble down the rocks with impressive speed.

I'm lucky I don't break my neck. The good news is, I make incredible time. I'd go so far as to say that I cut my time in half. I limp into the village just after dawn.

Panting, I decide I'll pretend that my encounter never happened. Met a dragon, hooked him in the nose, found out he was a little bigger than Yatanak claimed. Was subsequently mauled by said dragon-turned-man. Ran away before claiming sex could commence.

Did all that happen to me? *Nope.*

A choked sound of relief breaks from my throat when I see my village. The pale light of dawn limns everything it touches and the cheery rose and golden hues have never been so welcome. At least, I'm thinking that until I see too many women amassed on the plains. Apprehension socks me in the stomach. Are we being attacked? *Again?* Maybe I should have kept under the dragon.

Why *didn't* I try to seduce him?

Because you panicked.

It was all so unexpected. I mean, how could I have prepared for the knee-high protector to be so massive, and then for him to turn into a man? A virile, sex-starved man?

Before it all happened, I would have boasted to anybody that I'd take a man-dragon if it meant we could secure safety. For a dragon's protection, any one of my tribe sisters would do it. Heck, they'd ride any unrelated healthy male for free.

I would have thought I'd be the same way.

Instead, I ran away from him. And the queerest thing of all? I'm being plagued with something like *guilt.* Not only for my brother, not only for my tribe, but for the *dragon.*

I feel like I've done him wrong. Having time to think on my way down the mountain, I kept replaying how he was working to give me pleasure.

I wonder now if I was too hasty in my retreat. In my headlong escape.

Feeling weary with failure, I hurry to the group amassed ahead of me. As I stumble closer, I see some familiar faces. The visitors—or attackers, since their purpose here remains to be seen—are the Middle Plains Tribeswomen.

Pressing a hand to the stitch in my side, I race up to the convocation. "What's going on?"

The group's attention briefly shifts to me, and Sorgenfreiya, the spokesperson for today, evidently, answers, "We're trading two hundred sheep to Middle Plains."

"TWO HUNDRED!" I gasp-shout. "Why on Venys would we agree to this?"

Sheep are our clothing—our shawls, our shirts, our dress shifts, and our blankets. Sheep are also our food. To part with fifty sheep is a considerable strain on our livelihood. *Two hundred?!*

"We're trading them because Middle Plains has a grown man of no relation," Sorgenfreiya says. "This is Hallar, the Middle speaker's brother."

"But two hundred sheep?" I cry. "What if what's left of our flock can't support us—what will we eat?"

"Grain," Fenna, another of my tribesisters, replies.

"See how long you last on that without running anemic," I scoff. I stare around at my tribeswomen. "And say this Hallar they're offering us can get us pregnant. That's great—but we'll only *starve* with his baby in our bellies. Plus..." I narrow my eyes. "Is he proven?"

The Middle speaker's mouth firms.

I suck in an indignant breath and look back to Sorgenfreiya, furiously whispering, "He's a virgin? You know we should wait for a proven man! What if he only produces girls?"

Loudly, Sorgenfreiya responds, "Middle's speaker says this man's father produced almost nothing but sons."

"Says a *daughter* born of him," I say dryly. Then I shake my head wildly. "You can't agree to this! There needs to be a vote!"

"We have voted, Nalle," Sorgenfreiya explains, and gestures to our tribe. She gets closer, whispering, "Now that your brother has been stolen, we've lost our chance for a solid trade opportunity. We have to make a barter, and we may not get a better chance than this."

Suddenly, a scout screams, "WE'RE UNDER ATTACK!"

Every woman's hand reaches for her weapon.

I reach for my hip, but I have nothing. I don't even know at what point I dropped my knife. Is it halfway up the mountain? Is it lost on the floor of the dragon's cave, along with my good sense?

"Who's raiding us this time?" someone shouts.

"The Tribe of Giants!" comes the scout's reply. "They're at the boys' lodgehouse!"

My heart falls straight to my feet.

The boys are literally that—boys. These aren't youths turning into young adults. These are children who, yes, happen to be male—but they still need their mothers, their family. They aren't ready to be traded for siring duties, let alone *stolen*.

And the Tribe of Giants can best us. The women proudly reside in the Steppes, and as their name implies, they are indeed massive in stature. Their men were once said to be thirteen feet tall—and I believe it. The women of their tribe nearly are.

"I need a weapon!" I call to my tribeswomen.

A bladed cudgel sails to the spot between my feet, slicing into the sod.

My eyes shoot up to see that the Middle Plains women have raced to circle their man, their weapons raised. One of the women jerks her chin at me, her eyes dropping to what she's gifted me with.

I crouch, heft up the cudgel hilt, and rise, tossing her a harried, "Thanks! I owe you a favor if we survive this!" as I sprint to protect the boys' lodge.

I leap on the first giant of a woman that I come up behind, catching her tightly under the throat with my forearm, cutting off her air and clinging to her back like a demented monkey. I hold the cudgel tightly in my other fist, prepared to blast it into her head if she tries to bite me.

Anger burns behind my breastbone. The ladies of the Tribe of Giants were once friendly acquaintances if not allies. I *know* some of them. Every summer, tribe children of similar age groups played together when the North Plains and the Giants Steppes tribes met to trade goods.

With my face squished to the braids of the Giant's blue-dyed hair, I notice a scar on her temple.

I've seen this scar before.

I'm choking Glaive. When we were children, she took a boar's tusk to her face. She was lucky; she lived and the tusk glanced her and missed her eye. While she was recovering, we used to sit, sharpening our spears side-by-side. Heck, we sat beside each other and exchanged blanket weaving patterns too. I once traded her a set of timbrels for a *sring* flute. She was an honest person then, and fair. "What are you *doing?*" I shout at the side of her skull, ignoring the melee around us. "This isn't right! You're stealing *children.*"

Her hands succeed in ripping me down from where I'm clutching her with everything I've got. I land hard on my rear, the grass cushion not enough to keep the breath from getting knocked out of me.

"We need a man, Nalle!" she pants, looking down at me with something related to regret. "We haven't had a child born to our tribe in years. Some of us are getting so old we won't be *able* to have children if we don't hurry." There's a desperation in her violet eyes. She extends her hand to me, offering to help me to my feet.

Still sucking at wind, desperately trying to think of a way to stop the raid, I take it.

Facing off with her, I see my tribeswomen with their backs to the boys' lodge—and Glaive's tribe has us surrounded, every woman looking grim but determined.

Thankfully, no one is bleeding yet. But we're no match for women of this size and skill.

"Look," Glaive shouts over the din of a hundred charged voices. "We'll take good care of them. No one will trade us men, so we're going to raise up boys. We have to. We don't have a choice, Nalle. It's not like a man is going to just drop out of the sky—"

The whole earth shakes behind me as if a boulder has been catapulted to land at my back in the middle of the bare plains.

Everyone around us screams.

Seeing the opportunity to add my body to the wall of tribeswomen guarding the boys' lodge, I push forward into the fray, shoving between towering women three times my height. "Back off! Let's *discuss* the situation. No one needs to die today!"

I don't make it two steps before the Steppes women scramble. They scatter away from me looking terrified.

Surprised, I try to recover quickly. I bring my hand up beside my mouth. "Good! Run! Glad you chose... to retreat... from..."

Steam billows against my back, ruffling over the top of my head and past my sides.

Just in front of me are, oh, twenty-five terrified faces, all belonging to my tribe.

"There's a dragon behind me, isn't there?" I ask with dread.

Stunned silent, they still stand sentry at the boys' lodge. Brave of them. To answer my question, they nod.

I don't turn to face the dragon. Technically, you could say that I draw him away from the boys' lodge, and from my fellow tribe ladies.

I run like the dickens.

An infuriated roar blows up behind me—and then the dragon begins chasing me through the village.

Chickens squawk, sheep scatter, dogs bark, women scream, goats cry out.

The dragon shouts, *"STOHP!* Pestiferous feemale, I wyll keeyp yoosayf! I *dehmahnd* yoo kaahm toome!"

Lungs burning, I dive over the first fence I see... and regret my decision instantly.

Feathered wings slap at me and fifteen sinister hisses and unbelievably loud honks make me go deaf.

I've landed in the damn goose pen.

"Cripes! Get! *Off* you! *Mean* birds!" I screech, ducking my head and covering myself with my arms, receiving pinches everywhere as I'm knocked about, being beaten with wings that leave deeper welts than a leather belt.

Whummpf!

Heat seethes around me. Immediately, the scent of broiling goose-flesh hits my nose.

Goose shrieks and the sound of webbed feet slapping on soggy ground register to my ears—but hey, I *do* hear the chaos, meaning my poor ears haven't gone tits up despite the abuse.

(Some of the roasted geese disappear from where they fell around me. I ignore this because I don't care that they've been turned into dragon snacks.)

That is, until I'm hauled up and away from the ganders and geese who've assaulted me.

I'm dropped without ceremony between the dragon's sharp-clawed feet. Feathers puff up around me, softly falling back to the ground. The dragon doesn't let go of the back of my tunic where his teeth have me in an unbreakable grip.

Västra, a gentle-hearted tribeswoman of mine, rushes up to the goose pen and hauls out a white bird with wildly corkscrewed and curly feathers, perhaps the only damn bird who didn't bite me. Sebastopols are nice like that. "Ingrid!" she cries in relief. "You're okay!"

"Sorry, Ingrid," I say to the bird tiredly. After my flight down the mountain in the dark, not to mention my trek up the feckin thing, I'm beat—and from more than just goosewings. "I think your gander got toasted. Hope you pair with one who isn't a right bastard next time."

Västra gives me a dirty look (she loved Ingrid's gander too) but then her eyes swing to the beast behind me, and she backs away, her goose making all sorts of noise where it has its neck tucked under her arm, likely telling her how awful the goosecarnage was.

With a fortifying breath, I look up at the carnage-maker, who's finally let my tunic go.

The dragon is staring down at me, his eyes peridot slits.

I exhale weakly. And then I'm up on my feet and I'm running.

...For about three beats of a beetle's wing. Then the dragon pounces on me, knocking me down flat.

Women from what sounds like the whole freaking plains let out shouts of alarm, but no one breaks from their positions. And that's a good thing: if anyone leaves the males unprotected to help me, it'll make an instant opening for the boys to be stolen.

Growling, sucking in breath from lungs that feel compressed from the dragon's foot keeping me smushed down, I shout, *"Where is Yatanak?* I need to have a talk with him about *'knee high!'"*

The dragon turns into a naked human man on top of me. He wrestles me up to my knees.

"Let GO of me!" I screech as he grabs me by my braid to gain more control.

"We arrr maytes—" he starts to growl *"—yeht yooran from me! Durrring dane gerrr! Yoocuudav behn keeled!* Bahd female."

His overlarge hand claps against my flank.

My whole body jolts. "DID YOU JUST—" I try to wrench myself free *"—HIT* ME?"

"Ooooh, old Yatanak's arm is going to get a workout tonight," one of my tribeswomen cackles. "I don't know about the rest of you, but I'm going to pretend I have this man giving me a swat for trying to run from him too. Unggh, I haven't had a man pull my hair like that in so long..."

Catcalls follow her words.

And abruptly, the dragonman's body heat and punishing hold disappears.

Because every woman on the prairie has leaped on the virile specimen of maleness.

"Good!" I huff. "You can keep that crazy bastard," I complain, straightening my tunic, dusting off my tingling behind, and picking feathers off of myself. I fiddle with my braid, easing the spots that got tight when he used it as my damn bridle. "Wait til you see what he's swinging. You'll change your tune!"

"Says you," Halame, my tribesister, crows. "I don't care if his jack-stick squirts volcanic tar—just look at the size of it!"

The dragonman is dragged to the ground and disappears under frenzied bodies. Women are climbing on him, fighting over him like he's got the last poker left in the world.

I grit my teeth. For some reason, irrationality is tugging me under its current; I feel strangely about the dragon. It's more than the fact that his arrival saved us from bloodshed (and it did, because the Steppes Tribe were unlikely to leave peacefully and empty handed. And there's no way we'd let our boys go without a fight).

No, I feel... *proprietary* over the dragon. Which is conkers. Yet I can't shake the notion that these women are fighting over what belongs to *me*.

Plus it's pretty awful to maul a person with sexual intentions. If that were a lone woman getting lost under a sea of men, it'd be a horrific sight. And it's this uncomfortable realization that galvanizes my decision. Growling to myself, my hindquarters heated on one side from the stinging slap the dragon gave me, I bring up my cudgel. I figure I might as well use the broad side and take out as many Giant's tribeswomen as I can while they're preoccupied. And if it helps the anaconda with legs, then it helps the anaconda with legs.

(Yes, I'm referring to the whole of him, not his one-eyed snake, although the description pretty much fits.)

A cloud of blue-licked orange bursts the air.

It's *energy fire*. I've never seen it; I always thought it was the stuff of stories. It *is* the stuff of stories—dragon ones.

Remember the old 'snakebite' punishment where someone grabs your arm with both hands and twists to friction-burn the skin? A burst of a dragon's energy fire is said to feel like that—only magnified.

Who knew he'd be able to defend himself with it in human form?

Women shriek in pain. Another ball of blue explodes, rippling the air, and women fall away from the dragonman.

Looking aggrieved, his hair mussed every which way, he rises to his feet, glaring menacingly at the women who probably felt him up a little, judging by the whimpered lamenting regarding the considerable steel in his pole.

The idea that they touched him without his permission disgusts me.

The fact that they put their hands on *my* dragon also makes me irrationally angry.

It's made the dragon angry too. Lip curled back, he roars, "GEHT GOHN. Leeve myy terrrtorrry!"

His speech is all hisses and growls. But the more I hear him talk, the more it seems he's approximating our language. He seems to concentrate extra hard on forming words, but then again, his lips are leagues shorter than they were when he was a dragon. No wonder he's struggling. Still... I think I'm getting the hang of understanding him. It's far easier while he's not full dragon; his voice is less raspy and a different sort of growl.

"What did he say?" June, one of my tribeswomen, asks. From out of nowhere, she's procured a small vial of cooling liniment, and she's applying it to the areas on her body that received friction-like burns.

"Does it matter?" one of the Giant Steppes women replies, rubbing her skin where it's puffed up and angry-looking from the energy fire. "We don't need to understand him to ride him."

One of the Middle Plains ladies, her cheek red from the energy blast, is eyeballing every inch of the dragonman's torso all the way down to his bulging thighs. She claps her hand over her energy-burned cheek, looking determined. "If you help us catch him, we'll share him with you."

The Giant Steppes woman snorts. "So we do all the hard work and you get all the fun? No. We catch him, he's ours."

HE'S MINE!

I don't realize that I've shouted this until everyone turns to me.

And then the man turns back into a dragon. This time, when he opens his mouth, he breathes real fire.

The women scream and start running. The dragon lets them escape. Technically, he herds them, looking stoic as he drives the Steppes tribe right out of our territory with strategically shot blasts.

The Middle Plains Tribe doesn't stick around. They take their man and get gone before my tribe can talk them out of leaving.

My tribeswomen stare after them, most everyone looking beaten and dazed. "There went our chance for a man," someone says sadly.

"I wonder what he would have felt like," Arkrona sighs.

"Are the boys safe?" I croak.

Sahlgren, staunching a bleeding wound at her head—one she got when the Giants' tribe began to advance on us, not from the dragon—tries to nod. "The boys' lodgehouse was never breached. And Cevilla kept Yatanak in his turf house. They were never the wiser that we have an adult man, even if he is decrepit."

Grimly, I nod to acknowledge that I heard her. "Good."

No one speaks as the dragon stalks back from chasing Steppes residents away.

He prowls right for me, only stopping to scoop up a handful of whimsically curled feathers from where they'd dropped from me earlier. They look stark and strange curling over his clawed fist against his jet black scales. He shoves them at me like a bouquet of flowers.

Tilting my head back, I cross my arms and meet his eyes, which are the same color as the flames you get when you thrust a new copper pot into the firepit.

A fiery, furious green.

CHAPTER 7

HALKI

"YOUR BREATH SMELLS like burnt geese," my mate informs me.

More of my breath billows against her as I hiss out an exhale. I growl, and by the way she shivers, she might be able to feel the rumble of the sound in every vertebrae of her tightening spine.

"Don't drop my feathers," I warn her. Then I catch her in my hands, making her clanswomen all scream.

"QUIET," I thunder.

They shrink back.

"Owwwgggh," my mate protests, and I ease my grip in case I'm squishing her where I have her trapped.

I carry her to where I initially landed in her camp, where I dropped her hairy hump skin and her short blade on the ground before shadowing her during the clan skirmish. When I take hold of her skin and weapon and press them into her keeping, she seems surprised that I thought to retrieve her belongings.

My wings sweep out on either side of me, and I flex them, prepared to take flight.

"Wait!" my mate cries, voice muffled until she discovers a gap between my fingers. "Don't fly me back to your cave! I need to stay *here*. I need to find my brother!"

Brother? Her sibling is lost?

I close my wings. The rustling must tell her that I've acceded to her wish because I feel her sag into my palm. "Thank you," she breathes.

Elevated as I am in my natural form, the aerial view of her encampment is surprising; a myriad of domesticated creatures are penned in various places, there are twenty-two lodges made of timber poles and oiled leather, and sixteen longbuildings made out of staves and sod. Each roof is thatched. Each animal pen is secured by a simple gate. Furthermore, there are the beginnings of an outer wall being erected with spike-hewn timbers, but the thing is barely three-quarters finished.

Humans are herd creatures, thus my mate is unlikely to be pleased if I spirit her away from her people. But if I claim my mate's territory, I'll have my work cut out for me. This isn't exactly the most advantageous and defensible settlement.

Perhaps her clan would be willing to relocate to the forests that ring Flame Pass. Not too close to our cave—I can't entertain my *own* family without wanting to push them off a cliff. I imagine that I won't feel any differently when it comes to my mate's people.

But for her, I will try. "Tell me about your lost sibling. Where was he last seen?" I find another pleasantly-shaped feather on the ground, and I gather it and shove it between my fingers for my mate to add to our collection. She fits the quill end with the rest of the strange spiralling string-like feathers, gripping them carefully in her fist.

"He didn't get *lost* lost. He was taken by the Qippik tribe. They're going to use him like a stud!"

She sounds deeply upset. My gut twists in reaction, and I glare around the plains, imagining a group of manhunters creeping up to steal male infants. "How old is the lad?"

"Nineteen summers," she says.

You can determine the age of a unicorn by the number of spirals on his horn. Thus, they refer to their passages of time as 'spirals,' which vary depending on how fast the individual grows a new tier. Crested Merlin dragons count their age by seasons or solars. Beyond that, I don't know how other creatures measure their accumulated days, but as there is only one summer per season, if I'm following my mate's meaning correctly, her brother is no boy. He's a man. A human man, and humans rarely form mate bonds out of necessity. This man has been brought into a camp of women who want to ride him endlessly for his seed.

"Do human males suffer from red moon fever as dragons do?" I ask. If so, for the month of the blood moon, he may not mind his plight. It would give me time to woo my skittish *drhema*.

There's a long pause. *"Fever?* Dragons carry communicable diseases?"

She sounds quite worried.

"Do you have shaft chancre? Is *that* what's wrong with your equipment?" she gasps.

Chanre? 'Equipment?' Confusion forces my brow scales so close they nearly touch. What a subject change. I thought she was worried for her sibling. "We do not have diseases. And there is absolutely nothing amiss about me. I'm a Crested Merlin. Now answer me. Are male humans driven with a wild moon-lust to breed?"

There's a very long pause as she has her turn eyeing me with confusion. "Moon lust... no! And he's got to be chained up somewhere. This is not the sort of tribe you enjoy your time with. He's being forced to service women who have a reputation for being cruel! I *have* to save him."

I myself would agree. However, there's a fair chance that my mate's sibling is not going to emerge with unrepairable damage from a brief stay of captivity. He'll likely be angry, but he won't be broken. "We will set out to rescue your kin at dawn."

She shifts on my hand. "'We?' You'll come?" The hope in her voice is tinged with awe. It warms me, bows my chest with pride—and resolve. I would do anything if it would please my mate.

"Yes, *drhema*. I will be at your side to rescue my new brother by affinity." My dragon brothers by blood would be struck dumb with disbelief that I'm claiming a human for a sibling, but I'm driven to do anything and everything to secure all ties to my female.

"We can't leave now?"

My wings sink to the level of the ground to deny her this, the only thing she's asked of me (besides ordering me to let her go and leave her be; those requests I will not hear). "*Drhema,* you could not have slept at all last night as you made your dangerous mountain descent. I know I got no sleep as I lost my mind trailing you."

"What's 'drhema?'"

"'My cherished one.' My mate. You."

To this, she falls quiet.

Since she also doesn't argue that she's not weary, I take this as answer enough. We'll both need rest before we journey in search of her sibling. Nodding to myself, I absently offer her another feather through the gap in my fingers, feeling pleasure lick my insides when she accepts it. And I ask what I've been pondering since she appeared. "How did you know to seek me out? Have you felt connected to me all this time?"

"Since what time?"

"Since I began watching you when we were hatchlings."

"You *watched* me?" She peers at me from between my fingers before her gaze moves blindly over her clanswomen as if she's seeking some understanding.

My tail whips back and forth, forcing her people to step back even farther from us, giving us the illusion of more privacy. I frown. "If you did not know I followed you then, why did you seek me out now?"

"You watched me? You *know* me?" She tries to sit up, so I raise my upper hand off of her. She stares up at me in disbelief. "I went looking for you because I wanted help saving my brother, and I want these raids to stop."

My mate came to *me* for help. My *drhema* came to me, trusting me to protect her. There is no higher honor, no greater show of confidence among dragons. I begin walking quickly, moving on three legs and carrying her on one hand.

"When did you watch me? And where are you going?"

"I came upon you the first time when you were in a tunic skin that matched the color of your eyes. You wore a shieldmaiden corset so new that the straps squeaked when you kneeled down to pick berries. I was nine solars, you might have been near that. And we are going to your lodging."

I follow her scent trail where it is thickest until we come to a longhouse that bears the heavy scents of several other females too. Former to my arrival (mere degrees of a sunspan, considering I just arrived), these women lived here with my mate. That's over now. I push my nose past the doorway's leather flap, and find wooden benches placed along the walls, with firepits set in the middle of the structure at various points, with cooking pots suspended over banked coals. Rushes from herbs and sweet-smelling grasses line the floor, and on each bench is a bedroll, with antler bone combs and other human-needs things spread over the surfaces, and I am pleased that this lodge will serve well as our love nest.

Reaching my neck in further, I snuff when I confirm which station belongs to my mate. Carefully setting her on her feet, I reach my hand inside the longbuilding and begin scratching with all efficiency, scraping everybody's belongings out but hers.

Protests ring out behind us.

I draw my head out of the lodge and twist my neck, my scales glittering as they flex under the sunlight. I aim a glare that promises a painful fiery punishment to anyone who desires to submit further complaint.

When I'm met with wide eyes and no one speaks, I snort and turn back to emptying our dwelling.

When a particular item goes flying past her, my mate hollers, "Hey! That's *my* rug!"

Carefully, with two claws, I pick up the item she indicated and flick it back into the lodge.

"Thanks," she mutters.

"You are welcome."

Once our human den is cleaned of possessions we won't want and have no need of, I take up my mate once more, pleased because, for the first krevk'd time, she didn't try to run from me. I tuck her close to my heart and I move to enter our longhouse. I hunch my shoulders and my back sinks low and I try to collect my body in a tight enough crouch to fit under the doorway—but my wings, even closed, are too wide to fit through. I grunt with defeat.

I change to a human. It's getting easier every time I call on the shift; a welcome thing because I intend to be in human form as often as I need my mate, and I'm feeling very, very needful of her.

But then my stomach lets out a growl to rival any throat-originated sound that I've ever made—in this human form or my dragon state.

"Dragon, are you hungry?" my mate asks. She eyes me. "Didn't you just scarf down half a flock of geese?"

Holding her in my arms, staring into her eyes, I ask, "What's your name?"

She blinks. "Nalle. My name is Nalle."

Purring, I repeat her name to myself, enjoying the way my heart reacts to learning it. "I'm Halki. And I do need to hunt."

Several emotions chase across her face before she smiles up at me. "Hi, Halki." She gently escapes my hold by pressing against my chest. I find myself releasing her simply because she indicated that she'd like me to do so. She makes a gesture to indicate the cookware. "In exchange for your help rescuing my brother, it's only fair that I feed you. What do you like to eat?"

I eye the pots in this place. Piled full, they won't do more than take the edge off of my hunger. I give her a polite nod. "I will have whatever you would prepare for yourself. I'll also step out for the quickest of captured meals."

Her eyes widen. "You can't make dinner out of any of our animals—only certain ones are meant for food."

"I understand. And don't fret, I won't eat any of the clan's livestock."

She sighs in relief. "Good."

Reaching out, I wrap my hand around the back of her head and bring her face to mine. "I will return, my lovely Nalle."

Her eyes drop to my human lips. "You think I'm... lovely?" she breathes.

Desire heats my skin. "You have no idea." I step back from her before I ignore my need for food and devour her instead.

Just before I reach the door to exit our home, I twist my neck so I can send her one last look before I take my leave.

Her eyes are fixed on my hindquarters.

I stop walking and try to turn enough to properly see them too.

Behind me, she makes a choked noise. "What are you doing?"

I frown. "I saw you gazing at my flanks, and I thought it was with admiration."

She sounds almost hoarse as she replies, "It... was." She clears her throat. "You could bounce a silver five-piece off your rear end."

I look to her. "I gather that a five-piece is money. I'm confused as to why you would throw coins at my back." I glance back down at myself, feeling a strain cramping through the muscle that attaches my shoulder to my short human neck. "What an odd view. Without a good long tail, my lower half seems somewhat plain."

"Your front half makes up for that in spades," she mutters.

"What was that?"

"I said hunt fast or you'll risk getting caught in the raids?" She clears her throat a second time, and her gaze skitters away from mine. "Good luck hunting!"

I smile at her, wondering at the way her eyes go straight to my mouth as I do. "Thank you for the well-wishes, my *drhema*."

CHAPTER 8

Nalle

THE GOOSE FEATHERS that the dragon collected are decorating my bench, looking like Otherworld flowers, all silky and frilly and pretty.

My gaze keeps getting drawn to them.

All my life, the best connection I could hope for with a man would be a fleeting encounter with a tribesman who I'd have to share between all the other women of my tribe. I would get occasional turns with him, and I couldn't hope to be special.

I'd be just like everyone else to him. Worse, I'd essentially be a job. A duty-bedding.

Now I have a man who will protect all of my people just to see that I'm happy.

He treats me like I'm his focus, and it's exciting in a way I never expected. It's almost... arousing. It affects me in a way I wouldn't have dreamed possible, couldn't afford to consider, knowing that I'd never have a man whose body would belong only to me. Who must see me as unique, worthy of his sole attention.

The dragon better be prepared for what he's stirring in me. Because the more time I have to consider the wild events that began the moment I hooked the dragon in his cave, the more I feel myself becoming persistently attached to the idea of having him all to myself. A fierce dragon who turns into a massive, muscled man. A man who looks like he wants to devour me, one who has pledged to help me.

He called me lovely. I bask in the dreamy feeling that hit me the moment he uttered the word... but I only bask for the moment and a half it takes for me to recall that I haven't brushed my hair today and I fell in the muck of a goose pen.

Eyes popping wide, I sniff myself—and grimace. Is the dragon daft? How could he have stood to even *hold* me?

"Nalle, you better take the world's quickest bath," I mutter to myself as I begin stripping and kicking more sticks into the fire under the water pot.

FACE WASHED, BODY SCRUBBED, hair dried and loose from my braid, my furry boots off and drying by the fire, a clean and herb-scented tunic dress on, I feel... feminine. Pretty, even. The dragon has been gone long enough that I start to wonder if him getting a whiff of me pre-bath made him decide not to come back at all.

While I bathed, our food cooked. Or reheated, rather, since the stew's been here all morning, but I'm still claiming cooking-credit. I got it to bubbling, so it counts. I'm just spooning the last of my portion into my mouth when Halki's head enters the lodge. He doesn't change from his dragon's form, and he stays with only his head in the doorway. "I have returned, *drhema.*"

Relief is sweet and jittery in my veins. *He came back. He's going to help! He thinks you're pretty—even when you should be tossed in a pond with a gob of lye soap.* "That's great," I say with a nervous smile. "Did you catch anything?" I tip my bowl a bit so that he can see into it. "I have stew warm and ready for you, if you'd like."

"I would," he confirms. "I'll just be one moment."

His head disappears, the door flap drops down, and then there's a horrible retching sound.

Shoving my bowl to my bench seat, his saved feathers poofing into the air, I race for the doorway. *"Halki?"*

I emerge from the lodge to the sight of the colossal dragon's back heaving as he sits on his haunches, shoulders hunched, long neck lowered, snout nearly touching the ground. His wings are closed tight to his sides—and his ribs stand out in a painful-looking way as he looses another awful, hacking cough.

This dragon will put fear into the hearts of all women who would try to come against us. He'll protect us. He'll rescue my brother. He's our saving grace.

My tribe's saving grace is vomiting.

And more worrying to me on a personal level, the man I just mentally planned an entire night-before-a-daring-rescue with in the hour he left me alone enough to think has fallen sick.

"Halki! What have you eaten? Was it poisonous?" I shout, worried.

From my vantage point, I watch in horror as something large and dark crests his tongue as he gags. His jaws open wide, and two thin flaps of nearly transparent tissue connect his lower jaw to his upper one at the creases of his lips. They stretch and flex and fold, following his mouth's movements.

The thing on his tongue sucks back into his throat when he inhales, starting the painful gagging all over again.

Visions of my protective, lunatic devoted dragon that I've called mine for less than a day go up in smoke as I watch him work to heave his guts up. Why is my dragon dying?

I race around him, trying to get a better look at what's wrong. He's hacking like he's caught a wishbone in the back of his throat, with that dark thing emerging further every time he retches, but not evacuating entirely.

"Are you *choking?*" I ask, panicked. I even hold my arm up, fingers splayed, like I might reach in and try to clear any obstruction from his throat.

But his rows of incredibly long pointed teeth gleam. It would be stupid to stick my hand anywhere between those jaws, and even that measure would only help if I could manage to reach far enough back to clear any obstruction.

Halki coughs again—and then he hurls up a massive oblong... *thing.*

It drops to the ground with a soft *coosh* rather than a plop. Instead of wet and glisteny like stomach contents or his very innards from the violence of his disgorging, whatever has emerged is compact and dry and... odd. "What... *is* that?"

Kulla, one of my tribeswomen, takes her hand away from her mouth so she can point at Halki's... whatever it is. "Is that a bull's nose ring?" she asks.

I can't believe I'm getting closer, but I am. I peer down at it until my jaw drops in disbelief. Then I turn a look on our dragon. "What is this? Dragon, did you eat one of our bulls?"

"No." Halki reaches out with his claws and takes hold of the lumpy thing he vomited up like it's precious treasure and not his rejected stomach contents. "I flew until I came to some livestock penned near Ember Pass. I found food to hunt there."

"Umm, Halki? It's not 'hunting' if you found them in a pen," I point out.

"Ember pass?" someone whispers. "He stole from the Giant Steppes tribe!"

Ignoring the chatter that flares up like water on boil, Halki stands, carefully lifts the cause of his near-death, and carries his cube of vomit to the lodgehouse.

"What are you doing with that?" I ask.

"Storing it with our things," he replies.

I turn to stare into the sea of shocked faces around me.

"That's his casting," Yatanak says, leaning on his crooked carved walking stick.

"*You,*" I utter with blame. "Later, we're going to have *words.*" I reach up and behind me and begin braiding my hair with deft, aggressive lashings, getting it out of the way in case I can't help myself and I stomp over to his grinning self and give him a strikedown.

Everyone's head swivels to look at our wise old tribesman—except for the dragon, who is very busy arranging his vomit chunk with 'our things.' He's still in his dragon form so he can't fit in the lodgehouse; rather, he's nosing his dried upchuck next to my bedroll. I find myself leaning sideways to watch how meticulously he tucks it next to my wrapped-up blankets like he's helping it snuggle with them.

I look back to my tribe. "I need a new bed," I announce. *Somewhere else.*

Several of them shake their heads at me.

I roll the end of my braid back on itself so it doesn't get loose without a thong to tie it back.

Halki comes up behind me, his massive head dropping to nuzzle along my shoulder, and my tribe eases back from us, clearly revolted that the recently puking dragon is touching my skin with his mouth.

"Ready to retire to our nest?" Halki murmurs to me silkily. He closes his teeth over the meat of my arm with only enough force to sting, not puncture. Then he noses the spot and does the same to my neck, nudging my head to the side to give him the access he wants.

Eyes wide as wagon wheels, I let him. I stare at my tribesisters in befuddled—shared—shock.

That is until Västra, who stands facing me with everybody else, boosts Ingrid the goose higher in her arms meaningfully. "He's grooming you," she says. "Like an imprinted goose."

And Ingrid is at this exact moment nomming her bill along Västra's hair, making whirring, buzzing noises as her bill clicks, wholly engrossed in her bonding task.

Meanwhile, my dragon's teeth make a scissor-sharp snap every time he moves his mouth, and he's making soft wuffling noises as he 'grooms' me.

Overwhelmed, skin singing everywhere Halki nibbles me, I look to Yatanak, who still stands with the others, watching avidly. "What is a casting?"

Yatanak's wrinkled face turns even craggier with his smile. His eyes are on my dragon as he replies, "There are tales of castings being very important to Great Cresteds. They store them."

"But what are they, exactly?"

Halki bumps my shoulder like he wants my attention. When I turn my head, I see he's waiting for my eyes to meet his. "They're the parts of meals that can't be digested. Therefore, our system compacts those bits and regurgitates the bricks." He glances over his long and many-spine-wedges back to gaze at where his puke brick is hanging out next to my bedroll like it's getting comfortable. "You wouldn't believe the treasure one can find in their castings."

"You're right. I wouldn't believe it."

As if he doesn't hear me, he goes on. "I believe that the bovine's nose ring is solid gold. Very pretty. A good gift for my new mate."

"What?" I hear one of my tribeswomen choke out before several of them rush to retrieve the suddenly-valuable brick.

Halki's glimmering black tail slaps down to block the doorway. He glowers until everyone retreats. "This is Nalle's and my nest. You will not enter it."

"That's our lodgehouse," Vrylee complains.

Halki's crest fans out, and the streaks that decorate it turn bright and dangerously red as his whole mantle begins to vibrate with warning. "You will not steal my mate's nest."

"She's been 'your mate'" Vrylee points out, putting extra emphasis on those two words, "for like a day. That's been our damn lodgehouse for years."

Halki's tail curls around me—

Ahhh! A giant snake! I allow myself *one* shudder before I stomp down my instinctive bolt of panic.

—and drags me close until I bump into his foreleg. "Then you've had plenty of time to enjoy it. Embrace change as you part with it. And know this: Crested Merlins matebond in an *instant*." His slitted eyes glow menacingly. "I adore my Nalle, so I will forgive your questioning me this one time because you are her beloved peoples." He transfers his warning look to everybody else. "But Crested Merlins aren't known for being patient. Don't make the mistake of assuming I will continue to be lenient."

He turns, his tail drawing me with him towards our 'nest.'

CHAPTER 9

HALKI

NALLE IS QUIET AS I join her inside our longhouse, me retaking human form and guiding her with my hand at the small of her back to replace my tail.

"Normally I wouldn't be inside until chores are done," Nalle shares faintly.

I move forward to collect our feathers that have fallen to the floor. To my delight, Nalle joins me, lowering herself beside me to help gather them all.

"What are your chores?" I ask.

"Everyone takes care of the crops and the animals. And when that's done, there's other work." She indicates a rack set in the wall by her bench and her rolled up bedding and our casting. "I weave on the loom."

"Loom?"

She glances up at me, her lips tugging up with a special sort of happiness. Pride, I realize. It looks different on a human face than a dragon's, but it's nonetheless a very pretty look on my Nalle. "Want to see?"

"I would like anything you would show me," I tell her, staring into her eyes. I blindly set the feathers next to my casting.

Nalle glances away almost shyly. She covers her reaction by clearing her throat and stiffening her spine, striding away from me and approaching her loom like she's going into battle. "It's a warp-weighted loom. See those rings?" She points to glazed rings made of stone or clay. Multi-colored strings loop through their middles. "Those are loomweights."

"Yes," I say. "What of them?" The glaze on the rings is very shiny. One of them in particular fired a very dark blue-violet, and I would like to keep it. I wonder if I'll be able to leave it on her loom or if I'll be driven to store it amongst our treasure collection.

Nelle grabs my arm and steps into me. And then she presses on my shoulder.

Staring at her in consternation, I yield to the pressure and move back.

This is evidently what she wants. She rewards me with another smile. "Stand here."

She's placed me on one end of the loom. She takes up a spot on the opposite side—and she hands me a stick.

"What am I to do with this?" I ask.

"Pass the shuttle through the weft threads like I just did until it reaches my side."

With difficulty, I tear my eyes away from her lovely face to try to focus on what it would please her to show me. "I wasn't watching your loomwork. Show me again?"

Her cheeks flush a darker shade.

Something taps my hand.

It's her shuttle. She's already traversed her maze of threading, and I missed it.

My gaze jumps back to hers. "I'm sorry. Your stick of strings isn't what I was watching this time either."

A breathless, self-conscious sound bubbles up from her. It's like a quiet little laugh, and it is charming. She reaches up and takes hold of my chin.

Is she going to kiss me the human way?

She turns my head until my eyes are in line with her loom.

"Krevk'd," I curse sadly.

"What?" She's still holding my chin so I can't see her, but I imagine she's shaking her head to clear it because she sounds refocused when she says, "This is what you have to do when you pass it back to me."

And this is how she teaches me to weave. She holds my face to keep my attention where she wants it to be. Every time she takes her hand from my head, my gaze moves back to her face. Her breasts. Her waist. The curve of her bottom in her lovely earth-toned clothing.

When she catches me looking at her, she's flustered.

She's captivating.

She's also wearing a necklace made of carved bones that is so intricate, I must keep it.

Thankfully, I'm keeping all of her so I won't be driven to claim it off of her. Ideally though she might agree to reside in the treasure pile we will amass together, the special place where I'll keep all of my precious things safe.

"Halki?"

She's staring into my eyes which means I've failed at loomwork and have been gazing at her again. "I'm sorry," I say. "I don't know if it's because I find you utterly enchanting or if the upcoming blood moon is affecting my concentration, but I can focus on naught but you."

"You think I'm enchanting?" she asks, her beautiful brown eyes searching mine.

"You've enchanted me," I tell her. I sweep my thumb along her cheek, enjoying the sensation of her smooth skin against mine.

"Is it because of the bonding?"

I consider that I was drawn to her long before she physically touched me and sparked the mate bond. It was long before moon fever was a consideration either. "I don't know why it is. I just know that I've been entranced by you from the moment we met."

Her skin stains a shade deeper, flushing with her human blood. Her eyes lower, and I'm not certain if I've upset her until I watch her mouth curve in pleasure.

I have pleased my *drhema.*

When she tries to hand me her loom stick again, I catch her by the wrist, bring her hand to my face, and kiss the backs of her fingers.

All five of them go limp, and before her loom stick can drop from the way they've gone lax, I catch it and clumsily pass it back to her like she needs me to in order to complete the weaved set.

Rather than beginning the next weaving line, Nalle clutches her loom stick to her chest and stares at me.

I nearly sneeze as the scent of nervousness permeates the air.

It's a distinct smell not unlike rabbit thistle.

My focus latches on to Nalle's lower lip as she draws it between her teeth, and her flat upper teeth bite into the pillow that her plump lip provides.

Simply seeing her do this makes me uncomfortably hard.

Probably the moon fever. If my mate were a dragon, we'd be twined together, celebrating the event's imminent arrival, mating like lunatics.

Just the idea of being tangled with Nalle, my strange human limbs wrapped around her, and her oddly beautiful human limbs clinging to me as I drive into her body—

Abruptly, I about-face and distract myself by checking on my casting. Because Nalle has proven reluctant to join with me, and coaxing her pleasure with touches as if she were a she-dragon was not entirely successful. I couldn't even manage to help her to her pleasure peak. She-dragons have refused to be further wooed by males who fail in this manner, and understandably so.

Resolved to properly pleasure her next time, I tuck my casting closer to Nalle's bedding. Oddly, it was shifted away from it, likely by Nalle on accident.

If I were in dragon form, and by myself, I might cuddle my casting against me to satisfy my sudden-sprung desire to care for a nest of eggs. As I have no eggs to tend to, and since Nalle is watching and it's a little pathetic to play parent to coughing treasure, I settle for adding more feathers around its base and pushing it even more firmly against the knot of blankets that smell like Nalle.

Your mate doesn't lay eggs. You'll never get to partake in incubation.

Humans bring forth life with the female doing all the incubation alone.

Gripping my casting between my hands, staring down at it but not seeing it at all, I snort. So what if my mate won't be laying eggs that I'll get to tend to with protectiveness and care? I will be protective and care for *her* while she is swelled with young.

The vision of Nalle in full swell...

"Halki? Is your vomit chunk okay?"

I frown and face her. "Your human term makes castings sound almost off-putting."

Nalle's brows jump and lower. "Yeah, it's my word choice that makes it gross." Her shoulders tighten then vibrate.

I stare in consternation. "Did you just shudder?"

She laughs. "I did."

"Why?"

"Oh, no reason." She moves to the wall and takes a bucket off of a hook. "I have a lamb that needs me to feed it after I milk it's dam. Care to come with me while I do my chores?"

I stare at her more. "You milk sheep? Do you *drink* it?" I'm a little aghast. Sheep's milk?

Nalle's blink is slow and her look is pointed. "You regurgitate your food—and *keep* it. You don't have any room to judge. C'mon."

CHAPTER 10

HALKI

"SHE WAS BORN ALL OF three nights ago so she still needs help learning how to drink. It's a little unnatural for them to take milk from a bucket, but it's that or she'll starve," Nalle explains while I hold the surprisingly hefty creature across my thighs. Following Nalle's instruction, I carefully dip the lamb's muzzle into the bucket of warm, creamy milk.

"Drink, you appealing little ruminant," I tell the newborn creature. "We slaved to bring you this."

A flock of sheep, Nalle informed me, would have been reluctant to let me near even if I were human, because sheep are sensitive to strangeness of any kind—let alone a stran*ger* in their midst. As a dragon changeling, it will be a long while before the herd accepts me.

We followed the nervous animals across half the plains—or so it felt—until we came to a corral. A sheepcote, Nalle explained. But rather than enter it like they're trained to do, the whole flock fled around it—clearly to avoid me—so that I had to stay back and allow Nalle to catch the ewe she needed. Once the animal was tied and being given incentive foods to make her stand still, Nalle milked her and eventually the animal let me approach and feed her, and then attempt milking her too.

It was a poor, poor attempt.

"Squeeze the teat," Nalle had instructed. "No, no. Grab it from the top and close your thumb against your finger once you've trapped the milk. Good. Now pull it down from the bag. You can be firmer than that. Let me rephrase: you're not going to hurt her. Grab it and squirt that milk out—there you go. Well done!"

I felt like I'd accomplished the nigh-impossible.

Now I hold the creature's offspring, who is all reluctance about suckling from a pool of milk rather than the source. "Why can't we feed the little one straight off its dam?"

"Because she rejected her. Most moms are great but this one is a bit dim. Every spring, she delivers her babies then she bunts them away. If we don't catch her when she's lambing, the baby dies because she won't clean it off or keep it warm or let it nurse. And sheep always deliver in the worst possible weather. If there's a storm, preferably with driving rain or frigid snow, then it's perfect. Wait til the wee hours when every-one wishes they were dead asleep and the whole flock goes into labor."

"That's horrid," I exclaim. I look around us at the truly mad-sound-ing animals. While the lambs are the color of a night sky, the adults are snow white with black legs and faces. They look fluffy-soft, but that's not the case at all once you get up close. In fact, touching them makes your hands come away somewhat greasy. *Lanolin,* Nalle explained. The scent wasn't unpleasant, and in truth, it reminded me of Nalle. She smells very sheep-ish, although she laughed when I told her so.

Looking at the herd, I'm unable to determine which of the sheep milling around us is the one we milked. I'm glad I wasn't born a lamb. The whole flock looks exactly alike. "Why do you keep the female if she's so poor a mother?"

"Because she's a decent milker. When a ewe has twins or triplets and can't keep them fed well, the bad dam's milk can supplement them. Plus, we can drink it too. And make butter."

"Butter? What is butter?"

Nalle's cinnamon bark-colored eyes gleam. "Ohhh, wait til you try it. We'll add salt to the milk and have you shake it into butter."

Shifting the lamb on my lap, I consider her offer. "I'm already growing famished just hearing this."

"Okaaay, back to work. No getting famished while holding the pita-sized morsel. And you just coughed up a bull! *Really?*"

"What is a pita?"

She gives me a firm stare. "Feed the lamb, don't eat the lamb."

"I won't," I tell her, and wiggle the bucket to entice my wooly friend. "You must be hungry. Try it, little one."

I dip the lamb's mouth in the rapidly cooling liquid, and this time, she begins to swallow it. Her long tail begins wagging wildly.

"What will we do after this?" I ask Nalle, fingers sinking deep into the tight mat of wool on the lamb's back.

"Figured I'd pack supplies for our journey. I want to be prepared for... for whatever we'll find when we get my brother back."

Her brother, ah. Of course her mind is with her sibling. I feel selfish for only looking forward to catching rest beside her. Because I don't know her brother, I don't share her urgency to retrieve him. I'm happy to do it, but his plight doesn't consume my thoughts.

Not like the way fears for him plague Nalle.

"On foot, it would take days to reach the Qippik village. But with you, if you fly me..." she trails off, afraid to ask this favor, I think.

"I will fly you, *drhema*," I assure her softly. No matter what she asked of me, I would try to do it.

Her deep brown eyes shimmer as she gazes up at me. "Thank you."

CHAPTER 11

HALKI

WHEN ALL OF NALLE'S regular chores are done, she looks drawn. Even exhausted though, she is determined to see to her duties, and I admire her fortitude. By the time she allows herself to call this day done, she leads me to a latrine pit, a sandy little outbuilding set away from her clan's camp center. I follow her in, which seems to unnerve her at first, but then she disappears behind a half wall, crouching down, and I turn around to relieve myself against the pit's wall. It's an entirely surprising venture. I no longer have a cloaca that releases an excretory chalk smear fit for marking territory corners.

Instead, I find firsthand that a human male's sexual organ is also their excretory assistant, like an animal. How unconventional. It is long and wieldy and when I attempt to relieve myself, I spray water down my own leg. I have to grasp the rather sensitive handle and aim it so that I'm not spraying on myself.

The scent is pleasantly strong though. This will do well enough for marking. However, I now have concerns about what will happen once my meal is digested. If I'm passing only liquid here, what will happen to matter that I've digested? How does that exit?

"Are we peeing together?" Nalle asks, her voice sounding oddly strained.

"Now that I have the hang of this, seems we are."

Nalle makes an almost choked noise, but when I glance over my shoulder in her direction, she orders me not to look at her.

"I can barely see you above the partition."

"Don't look at me at all!"

Shaking my head at the strangeness of my new mate, I do as she orders and face my own business.

Finally, my water reserves seem to have reached an end. I shake my organ to rid it of drips, and enjoy the sensation of my organ being stretched and bounced. *Ha!* How do male humans get anything done? I could almost play with this all day. For being an open-air organ, it has a distracting amount of nerves and pleasantly receives the slightest stimulation.

"What the hell are you doing?" Nalle asks from behind me.

I turn, still holding my organ behind the too-sensitive cap. "Watch this flail. The length is ridiculous—here, why don't you try it?"

"What? No!" Nalle is standing, hands on her hips, brows drawn in, lips sucked between her teeth right up until I make my offer.

Then she's trying to retreat from me.

"Come here and take hold of it," I tell in exasperation. "It's not going to bite."

"I'm not going to touch it!"

From outside the latrine, one of her clanswomen calls loudly, "Then send him out and I'll touch it, you greedy cock socket!"

Nalle's spine straightens and she growls, "Back off, you she-jackal!" to whomever spoke.

I've reached her and because she was rebuking her friend, she must not have noticed my approach because when I bump her arm with my organ, she squeals.

"Do you need help in there?" another one of her clanswomen calls.

Yet another woman adds, "I'm volunteering too. I don't care if that man's in the damned latrine—I'll ride him."

"Perverts!" Nalle hollers, making my ears ring. "GO AWAY!"

When she turns so that she's facing me and not the latrine wall she was hollering at, I take in her nettled expression and my organ immediately fills up with weight, turning rigid as stone.

"You've waited too long," I tell her. "Now you won't be able to play with it."

"Give me five minutes with him and I bet I can make it play with me!" a clanswoman shouts.

"We need to get out of here," Nalle grits out. "Come on."

A pulsing need is burning in my lower belly. And I no longer want to play with myself. I want to play with *Nalle*.

She must see a change in me. Her eyes go wide and she begins to back out of the latrine. "Halki, let's go back to the lodgehouse and wash our hands."

"I don't want to wash," I tell her. "I want you."

CHAPTER 12

Nalle

THROUGH NO SMALL FEAT of will, I cajole my dragon to follow me while avoiding his strong, surprisingly skillful hands. We pass smirking tribeswomen who offer all manner of suggestions for what and *where* I should do Halki next, and I manage to ignore them as I lead him all the way back to my lodgehouse where I cinch the doorflap down behind us.

I fall back against the wall, heaving a sigh of relief.

"You're going to be walking bow-legged by the time he lets you out," Sorgenfreiya calls through the doorflap helpfully.

"Are you kidding?" Dunnah laughs. "Did you see the size of that club he's swinging? She'll be lucky if he doesn't split her in two, let alone if she'll be walking anywhere after he's done with her."

My eyes close. "Turn deaf ears on them," I huff. "All of them are absolute perverts."

"And proud of it!" Sorgenfreiya cackles on the other side of the flap before she finally leaves.

The graze of Halki's knuckle over the apple of my cheek has my eyes flying back open.

"I can close my ears to them," he rumbles. "Especially when I only have eyes for you." He drops to one knee, wraps his arms around my thighs, and tosses me over one of his thickly muscled shoulders.

I might have shrieked, if I'd had the oxygen. But the wind is knocked out of me the moment I get banged over this surprisingly hard part of him. There is no padding to his shoulder; not an ounce of forgiving fat to cushion his rock-hard muscle.

He marches us to my bench that serves as lodge seating and my bed platform. Without ceremony, he drops me onto it, and I do my best to ignore my proximity to his vomited brick, which is so close, it's nearly brushing against my leg.

"We shall sleep," he orders.

I exhale in a rush.

I begin unwrapping my boots, a process Halki finds fascinating. I unplait my hair and generally get comfortable while staying as dressed as possible. Then I scoot under the blankets on my bench.

Halki frowns—not at me, but the bench he expects to share. "Too small," he mutters to himself, raising his head and taking an imperious look at the lodgehouse's contents. What remains of them after a zany dragon all but hollowed it out, that is.

He stalks over (*so* naked, everything swings) to someone else's bench and appropriates it, lifting it like it isn't made of heavy planks of timber. But when he sets it down against mine, he isn't satisfied.

He grunts at it. "No bedding."

"We have mine—"

"Not enough," he declares firmly.

I widen my eyes at him. "How much do you need?"

"*We* need a most comfortable nest." He prowls to the door and draws the flap back, glowering when he receives whistles and rowdy shouts.

The gawkers are enjoying his frontal show probably as much as I'm appreciating my view of his behind.

"We require bedding," he informs them stonily.

"I volunteer!" several voices shout.

"I'll bed you anytime," comes another offer.

"*Blankets.* We need *blankets,*" Halki clarifies with a glare, crossing his arms over his chest—which only accentuates the thrust of his hips and the placement of his wide-set feet. His back muscles tighten too, and I'm struck dumb and drool a little as I ogle him shamelessly without him knowing. His body is lithe and powerful and proud.

And my tribeswomen are salivating for him.

Heck, *I'm* salivating for him. Are we really going to sleep beside each other and do nothing else?

I'm so busy wondering if I can keep my hands to myself that I miss what's spoken between Halki and my tribesisters, but he gets his blankets. He slaps the door flap down and his feet pound the floor as he makes his way back to our benches.

He's muttering to himself. "Those females are in desperate need for male attention."

"They are," I confirm. "Know of any single males who want to give them attention? Perhaps you have a brother or two you can toss to them?"

Halki pauses, a considering look flashing over his face. "I do have brothers I would feed to these she-sharks."

"Really?"

He clucks his tongue, in agreement I guess, and he rolls out the blankets he demanded until he's basically satisfied. He still says we don't have enough for a proper nest, but he says this will do for tonight.

With that, his thigh bunches, and his knee mounts the bench.

Where else am I supposed to look? Of course I'm staring at his front and center. My mouth has gone dry. This dragon is *hung.*

Halki's warm fingers cup my cheek, making me jump. My eyes guiltily fly up to his to find he's staring down at me with something both pleased and almost tender. "Your gaze, *drhema,* is more rewarding than all the treasure I've caved in a lifetime."

I'm sure I heard him correctly but I still don't understand. "'Caved?'"

"Collected. All treasure is stowed in a cave. Thus, we say *caved* to mean gathered and stored."

"Ah. Who knew?"

"Dragons." He rises up on the bench, fully kneeling on it now with both knees and an open lap, and through a supreme effort of willpower, I keep my gaze on his and not what he was trying to get me to touch earlier in the latrine. "Let us be well rested over the night so that we will be fresh for your sibling's liberation on the morrow."

Immediately, my thoughts fill with Jöran. I swallow, feeling my face bump Halki's hand with the movement. "Thank you again for agreeing to save him," I start.

Halki moves over me, closes his arms around me, and hauls me up until we're chest to chest, our gazes locked. "My mate has asked me for help and I will give it. Thank me no more, *drhema.*"

'*My cherished one. My mate. You.*' It's hard to wrap my head around how quickly I went from single, *normal* tribeswoman to being mated to a dragon, but I'm less and less shocked every time he refers to us this way. As he draws us down on our sides and strokes his big fingers through my hair, the more and more I'm embracing the concept of Halki being all mine for as long as we live.

Then Halki lifts his hand from where he had it wrapped around my middle, and he reaches over me to position something at my back.

I close my eyes and try to will myself not to comment on it, but my effort gets overridden by my pesky aversion. "Did you just make your casting touch me?"

I twitch when surprisingly soft lips make contact with my forehead. "Yes, and here are our feathers." He spreads all the little feather-rinds down on me, the curly Sebastopol's leavings becoming a decoration all over me as he draws a blanket over the both of us and murmurs a pleased, "Good night, my precious *drhema.*"

Something about his voice and his endearment fills me up so nicely that I sigh and snuggle deeper under the blanket, bumping against his hard, warm body which feels reassuring and *good*—and do my best to block out the vomit brick at my back.

Dragons are two cranks past insane... but they're nice.

CHAPTER 13

Nalle

WE'RE UP BEFORE DAWN. Halki lights the wick of a candle by puffing a burst of flame on it, which succeeds in lighting the wick, but also melts the tallow of the candle, sending the hot wax splattering on his arm and hand.

"*Krevk'd!*" he hisses.

Eyes blurry with sleep, I sit up in a rush. "Are you all right?"

He chuffs and glances at me. "Yes, I'm fine." He turns his limb, examining the wax that's drying on him. "It surprised me more than it did any damage. Thankfully, my scales must do some protecting. More than a regular human's skin, I'm sure."

I rub at my face. "Better your arm than any other free-swinging part of you," I mumble.

Halki barks a laugh. He hauls me up, shocking my eyes open, and draws me right to his face.

He plants his lips over mine and inhales.

I try to fit my hand between our mouths. "I need to use my tooth stick," I warn him. "My breath must be terrible."

His nostrils flare. "You smell good to me, *drhema.*"

My belly warms but I plant my hands on his shoulders and urge him to release me.

He does. "I need to visit your latrine. Will you join me?"

79

"With or without you, that's my first stop," I say, yawning behind my hand.

Halki takes my other one to help me off the bench. It's such a gallant gesture—one I've never seen the likes of. Men don't need to assist women *any*where. If they did, we'd be in a pretty hopeless situation because it's not like there's a helpful man waiting around every corner. It's lucky if you have one helpful man in all of your tribe.

I stare up at Halki, really feeling that he's not only a helpful man—he's *my* man.

"I don't know why you're looking at me thus," Halki utters in a deep, rough-edged voice that makes my lower spine sing, "but keep your attention on me this way and we'll be late retrieving your brother."

I'm ashamed at the split-second pause—but I break eye contact.

Halki exhales a breath into my hair, his mouth close enough to brush my crown. "Let's relieve ourselves and prepare to be on our way. The sooner we complete our journey, the sooner we can be joined here."

Taking his hand, I tell him, "I like the sound of that."

We walk hand-in-hand to the latrine. It's too early in the morning for anyone but the tribesisters who are sentrying as shepherdesses to notice us, and they're too tired to care about the still quite naked Halki strolling with me through the village like the breeze and morning chill are nothing on his excessive assets.

This time, Halki doesn't offer for me to touch him when we enter the latrine, and he takes control of himself fine, loudly making a steaming stream against a support pole as I pass him on the way to the pit in the floor.

After we finish, I'm more awake thanks to the brisk walk to and from my lodgehouse, and it's quick work after that to wash up, change to journey clothes, and grab packs.

"Should we tell the others that we are leaving?" Halki asks.

"We'll do it now," I say distractedly. "We need to get you clothes."

Halki jerks back like I've... well, like I've recommended that we bind up his lower half, which is what I'm suggesting. Or at least cover him so that he's not hanging out like he is.

"Clothing?" he chokes out. "Why? It will only be lost when I change."

I huff. "Fine, but when you're in human form, you need to start wearing a loincloth or something. We'll get one from Yatanak."

We do get one from Yatanak, but Halki's disapproval is thick and implacable. Also, him fitting on the tiny scrap of cloth doesn't lessen the tribe's bawdy reaction to him. To be fair, there's still so much of him on display.

"We're leaving," I tell them. "We're getting Jöran back and—" I have to raise my voice over the din. No one wants to send me off alone.

"She is not alone; she has *me*," Halki reminds them—and with that, he shifts into his dragon form, sending his loincloth fluttering to the ground. Nostril shields flat against his snout, he retrieves it by pinching it between his claws and holding it out to me like if I'm going to make him wear this, then I can be the one who carries it around.

I shrug and stuff it into my pack. Then I clap my hands together and eye his shoulders. "Time to ride a dragon."

Halki snorts and catches me between his hands. "Not until we practice thoroughly. For now, I will carry you this way."

And with that, we set off.

WE BURST INTO QIPPIK tribe's village only to find... emptiness.

There are fires with still-warm coals. There are animals who look freshly fed and watered. But no one is shepherding them. The lanes between sod houses are silent, and not one person is in sight.

The village is so much smaller than I imagined too. There are maybe ten sod huts, all smaller than any one of my tribe's lodgehouses.

And everything is so clean and orderly. There aren't bones scattered everywhere, the remains of men and boys lying desiccated under the hot sun.

If I didn't know where we were, I would think the settlement looked peaceful and—I curl my lip to think it—*nice.*

Halki shifts into a man.

When I glance up at him, he shrugs. "Easier to move this way."

Without a word, I pass him his loincloth.

He grimaces and brings it around his hips like I've handed him strips of slimy raw bacon, not fabric.

I almost snicker, but I'm too on edge. Together, we creep further into the base of evil, peering into sod houses, seeing clean, well-kept dwellings with absolutely no one inside.

"This is creepy," I whisper.

"I smell a scent reminiscent of yours. Male. Up ahead," Halki shares. "I think it's the grass-house on the left."

The largest sod house in the place, he means.

I'm breathing through my mouth by the time we've slinked up to it, my chest wall is taking a beating better than the stretched top of a goblet drum, and sweat has broken out all over me. *Where is everybody and what have they done to Jöran?*

Halki jerks his head at the door, a silent question in his gaze.

I gesture for him to knock it open.

With a surprisingly violent kick of his bare five-clawed foot, he does.

Muffled screams ring out as Halki and I force our way inside and find—

Jöran, *naked,* in the middle of tying a furious also-naked woman up. Except he's not simply tying her hands and feet. No, he's done disturbing things with the rope, making it cross over her breasts and running it between her legs and his fist is wrapped around two lengths of it that stretch tight over a very specific part of her crotch.

This is an erotic-flavored capture.

"Eww," I whimper, covering my eyes. "I'm not seeing my brother like this, I'm not seeing my brother like this..."

"Here," Halki says with a huge smile. "Take my loincloth."

"Thanks," Jöran mutters, taking it. He's staring at Halki and then at me, and then back at Halki.

I cast my eyes around us while he puts the loincloth on, and I see why the village is empty. *All of the women must be here.* The youngest is maybe eighteen, the oldest maybe Yatanak's age. Each and every one of them is tied up in a similar manner to the woman Jöran is currently paying attention to, and *all* of them aren't wearing a stitch.

Not unless you count the hemp rope. And ugh, the friction they must be feeling...

But they took my brother. He's *naked,* for goodness' sake. If they're uncomfortable, they deserve it; they deserve whatever he's done to them. I clear my throat. "Jöran, this is Halki—"

"We are mated," Halki informs him with an impressive amount of threat for as levelly as he delivers the news.

"—and we're here to rescue you," I finish weakly.

Jöran looks between us. His mouth quirks, and he sends me a smile. "Thanks, Nalle." He reaches out and ruffles my hair.

I'm having trouble processing. "I saw this all going differently. I thought you'd desperately need our help to get free and come home."

My brother laughs softly. "Why don't you help me round up my women instead? I'm missing two."

"Your women?"

Jöran smiles, and it's a masculine, powerful thing. For the first time, I really *see* him. Not as my little brother that I've always protected. Not an innocent brat of a boy whom I love to over-mother. A man. Jöran is a full-grown man.

With debauched pride evident in his voice, he says, "Meet my naughty harem."

I want to shudder at his words. But the evidence is all around us: these women did not get in this state because they were making wholesome appleleaf tea with him.

Apparently, whatever they were doing to land them here in ropes is the result of my brother teaching said harem a lesson. My brother flashes a raffish grin at two dozen sets of disbelieving (and some furious) eyes. "I warned you to behave."

I wave my hands in the air. "So you're not desperate to escape them? What about the young men they left dead on the plains?" I wheeze, thinking of those bodies, disgusted that I'm feeling relief because that fate wasn't also my brother's.

Jöran loses his smile. "What was done to those men wasn't what you think, Nalle." His gaze bores into mine before he gestures to a group of girls that I didn't realize were even here. He's left them untied, and they're huddled together behind everyone else, looking terrified of me.

I shift in surprise—but none of their attention moves with me. Oh. They're terrified of Halki behind me. I glance up at him to see he's hulking over me a little, and with his strange eyes and his scales instead of regular skin, he does look a little frightening.

I silently snort to myself, thinking, *You should see him when he's full dragon.*

Jöran continues, "No one bothered to ask my women why those males were staked out to die. Know this," Jöran's face turns harder, colder, "they deserved to be left out for the jackals to pick clean."

And then my brother is enveloping me in a hug. And for the first time, I acknowledge the bulk he has to his body. He's muscled and full-framed and taller than me by a head and a half and he's... all grown up.

Jöran isn't my 'little' brother anymore.

I suppose he hasn't been for a long time.

He draws away, giving me a gentle smile. "Thank you for storming to my rescue, Nalle. And I'd appreciate it greatly if you can help me tie up a couple of loose ends."

A few of his women growl, making his smile widen.

"Let's go find my troublemakers," Jöran says.

CHAPTER 14

HALKI

WITH MY SENSITIVE NOSE, we have no trouble rounding up the two women hiding from their mate. I find them in a little house covered with grass and dirt, and it's no trouble to step inside and raise a wide, flat platform that holds a down-filled bed, revealing the two females flattened underneath it like pillbugs.

Nalle's brother chuckles as he hunkers down and pets one of them. Then he catches them both by the wrist and hauls them up.

They spit at him and struggle, but at no time are they afraid of him. (Afraid of me, yes, at least initially. But not of their mate.)

Nalle seems shellshocked as she watches her brother haul one woman over his shoulder and spank his hand against her flank, making her scream obscenities. To his other female, he smirks and crooks a finger.

Mutely, she slinks up to him—and Nalle's eyes go wide when her brother leans down and roughly takes the woman's mouth.

Her fingers dig into his sides and they only break apart because the woman draped over his shoulder smacks him on his hindcheek.

"When my sister leaves, I'm going to make you apologize properly for that," Nalle's brother warns/promises his woman. He turns and carries her out of the hut, keeping his other woman secured by linking her fingers between his.

I like the look of the hold. I reach out to Nalle and knit our fingers just the same.

Nalle glances at me sharply, but then her expression softens, and she sends me an overwhelmed smile.

When all of Nalle's brother's harem is where he wants them to be, he turns to his sibling and places his hands on her small shoulders. "I think you've picked up on the fact that I want to stay here."

Nalle blinks up at him, reluctance warring with a bit of disbelief and a lot of shock.

"I'm happy here, Nalle. I can see you're struggling to understand how that is, but just trust me. I have this all well in hand."

"In damned ropes, more like it," one of his women mutters behind him.

His grin flashes for us to see, but his voice sounds dangerously low and full of warning when he responds without glancing back, "I told you what would happen if you spoke without permission."

The woman's eyes flash like a scorpion—all sting and killer glare—but the woman's scent thickens with arousal.

Nalle shudders, making her brother chuckle and pull her to his chest for a quick hug. Then he releases her and looks to me. "So. You say you're Nalle's... man."

"I am," I say firmly. My gaze is locked with his.

"He's a dragon," Nalle shares.

"I gathered that from the scales," her brother says. To me, he levels a dead-serious look. "You'll treat her well?"

A woman who's plucking at the knot situated between her forearms mutters, "Like you're one to talk, you sadist—"

Nalle's brother clucks his tongue and wags his finger at her, making her drop the knot and hiss.

"You don't seem surprised that a dragon can turn into a man," Nalle informs her sibling.

"That's because I'm not." He gestures to his harem. "My ladies are full of stories."

"You don't even look surprised that I'm mated to a dragon," Nalle continues.

Her sibling winces. "I've kind of got a lot going on right now, Nalle. And a lot of those things are tied up at the moment."

His women grumble, making him stifle a grin.

"Aren't you..." Nalle starts before she stops and shakes herself as if chilly water has spilled down her neck. "How long do you think you can service this many women all by yourself?"

Her brother scratches his puffed chest. "I manage them rather well, believe me."

"Arrogant dick," one woman behind him mutters.

His head whips around. "What was that? Maybe we need to put that mouth to good use."

Nalle shudders beside me again, and I wonder why.

Then she's straightening and seems to be coming to terms with something. "So... we're leaving you here?"

Her brother smiles gently at her. "This is where I want to be."

AFTER NALLE EXCHANGES hugs with her sibling, with her looking as if she's still half stunned, we leave the Qippik tribe, walking past their silent huts on our way to the plains where I'll shift and fly us out. I don't tell Nalle, but I spent a considerable amount of attention on the rope configurations I spied among her brother's harem. I like how quiet this kept his females as they busily tried to pluck themselves free, and I think Nalle's clanswomen could benefit from being tied up too. I'll be sure to tell my brothers this when I lead them to our camp.

I feel no guilt at the idea of feeding my brothers to Nalle's clan. I'm looking forward to it. "Your sibling looks well," I say to my mate.

"I guess he is."

"He seems happy."

"He looks it," she mutters.

I catch her by the chin, tilting her face up to peer down into her eyes. "Why aren't you pleased? You worried for your brother's safekeeping. Now you've seen he is fine. Explain your emotions to me."

"I..." she huffs. "I *can't*. I don't even understand what I'm feeling. I can hardly break it down for you."

"Try."

"I guess... this whole time, it's felt like an enemy took him away. They *did*. And I've missed him. And I was worried for him, and I thought when I got him back that we'd go right back to where we were, being a family again."

I shift to my dragon form and sweep my tail around her. "And now he's claimed a new family for himself."

Nalle sighs sadly, nodding.

I nuzzle her jaw with care. "You have me now, and I vow to you I'm worth a dozen brothers. Perhaps two dozen. Maybe more."

She snorts against my teeth, which are right at her face-level. "Speaking from experience, are you?"

"I am," I confirm, nibbling on her shoulder, getting hairs in my mouth from whatever creature's pelt keeps her shoulders warm. "I'd trade every one of my siblings for you, no hesitation. No quibbling. In fact, I'd like to bring them to your clan sisters."

Nalle draws back enough to stare up into my eye. "You're going to gift my tribe with your brothers?"

One side of my scaly mouth slowly curls up. High up. "Would you like to help me capture them?"

CHAPTER 15

Nalle

WE CAPTURE TWO OF HALKI'S brothers relatively easily because Halki doesn't tell them where we're going. Tamworth and Danelagh follow us out of curiosity because here their brother shows up to their mountain, mated to a *human* of all things, and he tells them they are needed.

I think we should tell them what they're in for, but Halki keeps covering my face with his oversized fingers every time I try. Bizarrely, he asks his siblings if they remember how they taught him to swim and fly. Evidently, Danelagh used to tell him he was 'refining Halki's technique' by tossing him off cliffs and watching him plummet to the ground. Tamworth has a gift for holding his breath long enough to reach great depths of the sea, and when Halki was young, this earlier-hatched brother captured Halki and dragged him underwater with him until Halki learned to dive too. It was that or drown.

The more and more the brothers laugh good-naturedly together over the memories of them torturing Halki as a nestling, the less and less sorry I feel for them about how they'll be entering into our village blind.

We have to make a stop when we're gliding out of Flame Pass because the dragons are famished.

Halki sets me down and sits beside me. I fit my hand on his side under his tucked wing, feeling like everything is a little surreal as I stand in a circle of dragons as they discuss luncheon plans.

As they consider various hunting options, my attention leaves them because I feel the bite of pebbles hitting my skin. When I bat at myself and try to pinpoint the source of where the rocks are being thrown from, I find a bachelor herd of satyrs on the opposite side of the pass.

When the otherlanders see that they have my attention, they begin miming lewd gestures to me.

When I don't react, they begin calling crude and vulgar suggestions.

I tap Halki on his foreleg, and when I have his attention, I point to the beasts. "Did you hear what they told me to do with my mother?"

As one, Halki and his brothers frown and turn their heads in the satyrs' direction.

"No," Halki replies. "I did not hear. But you can show me how to tan their hides when I gift them to you." And just like that, Halki is scaling the cliff, chasing after the satyrs who are scrambling up the side of the mountain.

He dines on goatman haunch and gifts me three satyr pelts. Danelagh and Tamworth happily bring me four more, also filling their bellies with satyr meat. I'm offered some too, but I decline in favor of eating when we get back to the village. I show Halki how to fold the wet pelt sides together and tell him that we'll need to stop in at the salthouse immediately so that we can treat the skins. It's relatively cool in the mountains, but it's still too warm to have any hope of saving pelts without the preserving salt.

When we arrive on the plains, Halki glides skillfully to the ground and his brothers land on either side of us. They stare at my tribesisters who look just as shocked to see three dragons in their midst as they were when Halki first appeared.

Halki calls to them, "These are for you." And he nudges Tamworth and Danelagh forward with his wings.

My tribe goes wild, rushing us.

Halki's brothers realize something is very wrong with this. They begin to scramble backwards but Halki's wings keep them pinned at ground-level long enough for women to surround them. Danelagh squirms out from Halki's hold and alights on a nearby rooftop, making the entire structure groan, and he coughs out a sound of sheer surprise. "What elven brew have I imbibed that I'm seeing this?"

"It's like being swarmed by lunatic rabbits!" Tamworth shouts, completely circled by women and still trapped under Halki's crushing wing.

"Speaking of lunatics," Halki says conversationally, "the red moon is coming. Have either of you selected a mate?"

"No," Danelagh replies from the roof, curling his tail around himself and extending his neck so that his nose hovers just above my tribesisters who are stretching up to touch his snout. "But I've been told we'll lose our minds with mate fever and we'll be forced to find a female or else go mad."

"Perhaps you'll find a mate among this lot of lovely females." Halki's wings shrug—which gives his trapped brother the opportunity to shrug out from under his pinning. Tamworth slides out and shoots into the sky, leaping onto the same roof that Danelagh is already perched on.

The roof caves in and the dragons crash to the ground.

They get swarmed.

When Danelagh (the brother who taught Halki to fly) leaps ahead of the throng and nearly escapes, Halki catches him by the back of the neck like a mother cat holds her kitten, and he tosses him back to my tribesisters. Halki smiles as he calls, "Danelagh, I think you're really getting the hang of this!"

...Which is apparently what Danelagh would tell Halki when he managed to return to the top of the mountain, shaking with exhaustion and shock after being tossed off the cliff for the first time that day.

I sort of want to stay and watch how their arrival plays out, but I'm feeling a little raw from the loss of my own brother. Because although Jöran did appear perfectly happy and he definitely appeared to be in control, not having my little brother in my life is going to take some getting used to. I trudge for the salthouse.

Halki falls into step beside me, and he seems to sense my mood because he nudges me more gently than ever with his big snout. "What ails you, *drhema?*"

"I'm going to miss Jöran," I admit, my throat tight. "Until he was taken, I've been with him every day of his life," I tell Halki, having to raise my voice slightly to be heard over dragon's curses and my tribesisters' excited shouts. Geese honk, sheep cry out in alarm as one of Halki's brothers breaks from the pack of women and busts through a pasture gate. He's attempting to find a wide enough space to extend his wings enough that he can fly, but my tribe latches onto him until he resembles a honeycomb swarmed by bees. Halki keeps his eyes on me, and I continue, "And now I'll never see him."

"That's not true. I can fly you for visits as often as you like."

I sigh unhappily. "Thank you. If the fall harvest is good, we might travel that way to see what his tribe has to trade from their harvest and visit with him then too. But it won't be the same. Like you pointed out, he's got a whole *new* family, Halki. He doesn't need me anymore."

"Ah," my dragon says, and his wings come around me. Oddly, they're thin enough for the sun's light to pass through them, turning the black surfaces to a nearly transparent pink, yet they're an effective enough barrier against noise that the sounds of two panicked dragons being pursued through our settlement barely register. "This, my tenderhearted female, is the nature of family relationships. Your brother is grown and needs you no longer. He'll still love you though. And now you have me, Nalle, and *I* need you. Forevermore, I'll need you. You can believe that."

I gaze up at him, hearing the seriousness in his voice. And I know that we haven't known each other long enough for the feelings between us to make sense, but Halki isn't alone in this: I feel as if I need him just as much. I only just met him but if he disappeared today, I'd be devastated.

I place my hand on his nose, my thumb brushing the part of his nostril where I hooked him. He's got a little hole in the thin scale. "I'm glad I have you, Halki."

His eyes glitter like green gems. "You do have me," he confirms. "And when you're ready, I'll demonstrate how much I'm yours."

I go still, thinking of his naked human form, with all of his glorious muscledness, scales and all. My eyes squarely meet his. "I think I'm ready."

Halki's eyes widen. "Are you certain? What of your duties and chores?"

I shake my head. "You're right. I'm not thinking clearly." I glance back up at him. "But tonight then." I'm certain I'll crash like a felled log after I'm treated to all of him, but there's no way I could hope to sleep tonight otherwise. My head is too full. "Honestly? I'd like you to distract me," I tell him.

My dragon purrs, the sound vibrating the air between us, sinking into me in rapid waves. "I will ever so happily oblige your wish." His teeth flash bright white against the backdrop of his dark scales. "I'm relieved at your timing. The blood moon's fever is going to have me crazed for you. Soon, I won't be able to think of anything but being inside your body."

I lick my lips, holding his gaze. "I'd like to get lost in that fever with you. Take my mind off of other things right now."

Heat flares in his startlingly green eyes. "My poor female." He shifts into a man and takes my hand. "Come, my mate. Let's salt our skins and spend quality time together in private."

I grin at how strange that statement sounds, but I reach into the salthouse and retrieve a bucket—which Halki insists on hauling back to the lodgehouse. "It is pretty loud out here, hard to clear a mind and concentrate," I agree, and we both ignore the pair of dragons hollering Halki's name like they're cursing it. "But shouldn't we help them before we go?"

"Who? My siblings?" Halki scoffs. "They produce the same fires that I do. If they wanted to escape your clanswomen, they easily could. Are you hungry?"

I gape at him. "You polished off a band of satyrs all of a sunspan ago. Are you serious?"

"You she-beasts stay back!" one of his brothers yells. We both ignore him.

Halki frowns. "That was half the sky from here. And besides, *you* didn't eat anything. Let's feed you and then I'll clean up your leftovers."

CHAPTER 16

Nalle

I'M A LITTLE ALARMED at how much Halki needs to eat. He found a pack of scrub jackals stalking our sheep and he ate those while I prepared roasted chicken for me. And as he promised, he ate my leftovers, acting like he wasn't already too full.

How will our tribe support *three* dragons? "Maybe we shouldn't drag more of your brothers here," I tell him. If they haven't already bonded to ladies in my tribe, we should probably let the two we have go.

"Nonsense," Halki scoffs, using his claws to pick membrane off of his satyr hide as he scrapes and softens it. He's smoking it with his breath as he tans it. I've never seen the process performed in this order before—and never in this way, using your own body's fire, of course—but if it works, dragons are even more handy to call allies than I could ever have guessed, or hoped for.

I intend to pay attention to his work and offer instruction as needed, but Halki's arms and shoulders and back are such a distraction that I'm hypnotized every time he so much as twitches. *Everything* on him flexes and I lose all faculties.

Unbeknownst to either of us, soaring high above the North Plains of Venys, a burning eight-tailed comet sears across the sky, blindingly bright streaks trailing behind it. It's beautiful, but it comes with a scarlet moon, the red moon of legend, and it sparks the dragon's mating fever.

CHAPTER 17

HALKI

ENERGY SIZZLES OVER me and sparks fire in my veins.

The club between my legs swells and tents the loincloth that Nalle insisted I wear for reasons understood only by her; it isn't as if this ridiculous scrap of fabric preserves my modesty, not with my hind cheeks covered more by suggestion than fabric.

As for the front of me, my instant erection makes a mockery of the covering, looking more obscene as it juts the fabric up and pulses in time to my thudding heart.

A wave of heat washes over me, making me want to turn, catch up Nalle, and seat her on my pounding staff.

Mating fever. This has to be mating fever. The red moon's effects must truly have begun.

I stay facing my work. With deliberate movements, I fold the wet sides of satyr hide together and lean over to sink my hands into the wash basin beside me where I scour myself all the way up to my elbows.

From the corner of my eye, I watch Nalle bring a hand to her heated-looking cheeks. Then she's running her touch to her neck, as if it too is hot. She glances at me, her lips parting, her eyes glued to my profile, and soon she begins to fan her face.

Ahhh, drhema, *do you burn in the fever too?*

If I'm not mistaken, her thighs clench. I wonder if she aches for me as I'm aching for her. My flesh throbs, and with a panted breath, I turn to look at her and find her ogling the vicinity of my hips.

Her scent carries to me then. It's bright and molten hot with desire.

Pleasure punches my system. My mate wants me—she's affected, just as I am.

This is also cause for concern because the fever will keep us breeding, even when our bodies might need other things. Such as sustenance. And while I've been driven to eat a little extra every meal, I'm not certain if Nalle has shared this drive. The good news is, a human body can go a month without food as long as she has access to salt and water.

I glance down at the salthouse bucket next to my satyr skins. Beside them are a dozen waterskins.

I smile. We'll be fine.

I turn and begin to stalk my mate.

CHAPTER 18

HALKI

BEING THAT MY MATE has a penchant for making me chase her, driving her to run from me should feel like nothing new. But it takes my interest and boils it, turning my hunger for her body into a beast. When I growl and pivot to shadow her, it makes my pulse hammer and her breeding scent intensify.

My body responds, answering to her call of need. I thicken even more, and my rod begins to hurt, I want her so fiercely.

Nalle's hair is in braids held by beaded ends, which slap and clack together as she dodges and dives. I chase her around the cooking pot, past various things that matter not and don't slow me down nearly enough to save her from me. She's in soft-tanned clothing, the kind that requires no pants and is easy to tug up or tear off, whichever I feel I have patience for when I catch her.

When I catch her by her hair, Nalle squeals and drops to the floor.

I follow her down, grabbing her upper arm and keeping a firm hold on her braids, bringing her neck back, baring it for my teeth to nibble and taste her.

I straddle her rear, making her squeak when my staff pokes and prods at her. The only reason I'm not sack-deep in her body is because of her clothing skins. I release her hair and fist her leather skirt, ripping it above her hips.

"Wait, wait!" Nalle cries.

"Do you have a virgin's barrier?" I manage to say through lips that don't want to cooperate. I realize my teeth are bared as I crouch over my female, pinning her for our first breeding. Through a desperate struggle of willpower, I shift my gaze to our benches with her woven wool bedding.

We should mate there.

Nalle is no dragon female to enjoy the scrape of the cave floor on her belly as she's stuffed full and ridden hard by my cock.

"I," Nalle gulps a loud breath. "I took care of my 'barrier' by myself, years ago."

"Good," I purr, and squeeze her smooth and silken hind cheek hard enough to make her gasp and squirm. "Great scarlet moons, these hindquarters! I could sink my teeth into them."

Nalle begins to pant.

"I'm going to carry you to the bedding platform," I tell her. "If you escape from me, I'll knock you down and rut you where we fall. Understood?"

Nalle's neck goes limp, her cheek making a slapping, sticking sound as it connects with the floor. "Yes," she gasps. "I understand you, Halki."

And then her hips wriggle. It makes her bared ass cheeks jiggle.

"We aren't going to make it to the bedding platform," I utter hollowly. My hand dives under her hips and she cries out as my fingers search for her feminine pleasure bud.

My first attempt at this wasn't successful, and I haven't forgotten it. But Nalle knows me better now, she trusts me, and she's giving off little signals in the hitching of her breaths, the rising of her hips, and her encouraging moans.

Of course, the concept of her having a main source of pleasure tucked somewhere isn't entirely alien to me. Female dragons have a bud like this too. Just inside their vent, their pleasure-organ engorges with blood, it brings them unbelievable delight to have it teased, and it's tucked into a spot that's a little tricky to manipulate.

I do well enough at manipulating Nalle's. I know this when she begins barking my name. Her body twitches all over, and I play with the soft, sensitive part of her until she's trembling and bucking and leaking heat-scented wetness between her thighs.

When she gets to her knees to offer her back to me for mounting, I know she's ready for breeding.

I catch her by the hair again, twist her neck to bare it for my teeth, and catch her by the nape in a stern hold.

"Halki!" she cries out as the blunt tip at the end of my shaft prods at her swollen folds. Each poke makes her breath hitch with excitement, and hearing her reaction makes me crazed.

My pelvis hugs the pillows of her ass, and it's a singularly comfortable and enflaming feeling. I want to pound against these and hear our skin smack together. I want to feel my hardness spank her.

When my shaft finds the spot where her softness hides a hot silken mouth, I sink my tip into her wetness, and drive deep.

My shaft's oil glands spurt the thickest fluid I've ever spent, easing my way and heating her insides to liquid fire.

Nalle screams my name, and I growl into her neck. *Damnation,* this feels like flying straight to heaven.

Her elbows buckle, bringing her shoulders-down on the floor before me, forcing my mouth to release her flesh else I'm afraid I'll hurt her. But that's all the concession I'll make, and because my fist is gripping her hip, she's forced to arch her back, because I'm not letting her get away. No, she's staying right where she is. I withdraw my length, reveling in the sucking sound her greedy sheath makes as my shaft pulls out of her body's erotic hold.

"*Ummghhm,*" Nalle moans behind her hands, still half-collapsed.

Chest punching her back as I inhale and come down over her to give her nape a nuzzling kiss, I find the willpower to take a slow glide through her tender folds, trailing my cock feelers, letting them go to work before I find that place between her lips again and sink easily back inside. I curl my hips against her hard, making her grunt in shock and shoving her body forward along the floor. There's a woven rug ahead of us, and if we aren't rutting in a bed this first time, I can fuck her onto the rug at least.

I pull out of her and slam back in, vowing to do just that.

CHAPTER 19

Nalle

HALKI'S MEMBER IS THE stuff of legends. It's tremendous.

The two strange feelers at the end of his staff elongate and wrap around my clit, tugging and tickling. Every time he withdraws, the tension eases up—and that's when they feather over me, making me bite my lip and moan at the sensation. When Halki thrusts deep, the tension increases until the feathers jerk off of my clit. It's a teasing rhythm that drives me wild.

The orgasm hits me like a surging tornado, making me scream.

"*Yessss,*" Halki hisses as his shaft is treated to a powerful massage. He stops thrusting and holds himself tight inside me to best take advantage of the way my channel flutters and grips him.

My whimpers and noises drive Halki to the edge. He begins hammering me, his hips pistoning with enough power to make me see stars, his release barrelling down on him.

But instead of coming, he pulls out.

Halki wraps around me like a land-attacking octopus. His strong body forces mine to roll over so that I'm facing him.

"Ouch," I complain when my elbow bangs the floor planks.

"Curses on dark elves! Sorry," he rasps. He shoves his arm under my shoulders and hauls me up until I'm cradled to his chest. Which is easily three of me wide. My face sticks to his scales; he feels hot as a braised bull's haunch. He leans us forward and snags a woven floor rug, setting me knees-down on it, his loincloth no barrier at all as his staff prods at my tunic dress (which has dropped to cover my lap) like it's trying to make friends.

I'm surprised to find that I'm no longer afraid of what Halki's utterly strange organ will do. Instead, I'm primed to experience it again. "Why did you stop?" I ask.

"Wanted to see you," he pants through bared teeth—and his gaze is devouring me. When he meets my eyes, his satisfaction is clear in his glowing green stare.

He takes a rib-launching breath and my eyes are drawn down the length of his body. He's beautiful. Scales and all, his strong body is a work of art—and he is *all mine*. Fire laps through my system.

"Nalle," Halki growls.

My eyes snap up to his.

"I want to skin you," he declares.

The longest beat of silence ensues.

I don't think I've ever blinked at anyone as much as I'm blinking up at him. And his face is so earnest, it's disturbing. "Don't repeat that. Just tell me you meant something else."

Halki frowns. His clawed finger and thumb pinch my tunic's shoulder strap. "Take this skin off."

A laugh catches in the back of my throat, but he looks so serious, I don't let it out. I should earn a prize for how hard I have to work to stifle my smile, but I reach for the fastenings on my dress.

"Wait," Halki says. "I want to do the skinning."

Eyes wide, I hold up my hands. "Every woman in the tribe is jealous of what's happening in here, but they have no idea what I have to deal with when it comes to you."

Halki frowns again. "Climaxes that make you cry my name?"

I nod primly. "All right, you can deliver those, I'll give you that."

He makes a disbelieving noise. "You'll 'give' me that, will you? The nerve, female." Under his gruff words, he sounds amused. And breaths coming in harsh pants, Halki slowly unwraps me.

A yearning look takes over his expression, and his gaze speaks to how fortunate he feels to have me. It sets my tummy on fire, combats my shyness, and dispels any vestiges of hesitation.

Manner caught between tenderness and hunger, he runs his fingers down my throat, between my breasts, over my belly, and down one thigh stained purple with his oils. It's shocking—not the staining; his patience—because I expected him to rush and rip at me and take me. He's wooing me after he conquered me, which feels backwards—but maybe this is the natural order for dragons: *bond to mate, breed mate, learn mate.*

Knees touching, his slightly trembling fingers careful, his eyes get hotter and hotter as he explores my body with touches that are so chaste they almost feel shy.

They make me *feel* shy. I find myself blushing under his starving, appreciative scrutiny.

When I glance away from him, Halki's knuckle hooks me under the chin and tilts my head up until I'm forced to meet his eyes.

He grunts.

He frowns and grunts again. Then he's scowling and showing me his teeth.

"What?" I ask, my voice shaking slightly as I try to suppress a nervous laugh. "Are you so caught up in passion that you've lost the ability to speak?"

Halki's eyes flash. Looking gravely serious, he nods once.

I blink at him. "Oh."

Learning how overcome he feels is intoxicating. He still hasn't cum; he's so swollen and hard between us that I'm amazed he's not howling from pain. He's leaking purple fluid onto the floor, but he's ignoring his jutting organ, keeping his focus on me, so I keep my focus on the rest of his body. Lighting him up everywhere else that I can. My hands stroke up his sides—and to my delight, he arches and purrs for me in pleasure.

There isn't really any need to remove his loincloth; as he's already demonstrated, he can get to me fine simply by flipping it aside. But I bring slightly trembling fingers to the ties of it anyway, and my insides turn warmer when Halki's skin flickers at my finger's touch over his hip.

Now both of us are naked, facing each other.

His wide chest fills my field of vision. He's so tall that he'd have to lean down if he wanted me to stick out my tongue and flick one of his nipples.

My tongue suddenly wants that. I wonder how he'd react. I don't think dragons have nipples in their natural form so teasing his should be an eye-opening experience for us both.

Chest rising and falling faster, my gaze traces over Halki's frame with proprietary satisfaction. His broad shoulders seem to stretch from one side of the building to the other. And the way he sucks in his breath and his abdominals stand out in sharp relief as my gaze sinks down his body...

My mouth goes dry at the same time the spot between my legs grows wetter.

Halki's eyes are taking me in the same way that I'm staring at him. His hand slides over my stomach with all the pressure of a butterfly's wing, as if a rough movement from him will make me disappear.

"Soffft," he murmurs on a rumbled breath, stroking me.

Well, my skin would be. Even in his 'human' form, his scales have a slightly abrasive quality to them, and his palm-scales are flat-out calloused. He strokes all the way down until he reaches my thigh, and then he slides his hand until he's cupping my bottom. He adds his other hand below my other cheek. And then he's hauling me against him, front to front, and carrying me towards the bed like the building is burning and reaching the horizontal surface is how we'll survive this.

He drops me on my back on the pile of our coarse woolen blankets—

I ignore the vomit brick which is nesting with the blankets. Which isn't easy because the damn thing has multiplied; Halki returned from his jackal hunt with an upchuck chunk of similar size but fulvous in color. The pair of them are brushing my shoulder and touching my hair, but I do my level best to pretend they aren't with us.

He moves over me suddenly, and with surprising skill for a man who's really a dragon, he expertly parts my legs with his knee. His cock bumps its wide, shiny crown against my mons, and the feathers at the tip tickle along my slit, slipping between my thighs.

Nothing could have prepared me for the strangeness of these two invasions. Wriggling wildly and *tickling.*

But the cries they haul from me are not complaints.

When Halki's face moves over mine, I tilt my head up to receive his kiss.

Instead, he shocks me by dragging his textured jaw against mine and... his lips find my earlobe.

He opens his mouth, gently draws my lobe past his lips—and then he bites me.

"Ahh! I thought this was going to be a *kiss!*" I start, my hands flying to his arms, squeezing his muscles here—and the hardness of them sends a punch of lust rushing through me.

Meanwhile, with a little lick, Halki releases my ear and begins teasing down my throat.

He fastens his lips, sucking at my neck—and then he bites me like a vampire bat.

"What are you *doing?*" I pant.

I can't imagine old Yatanak sucking on a woman's neck. Actually, I don't *want* to imagine it. But I have seen some evidence of such a thing. Plus, I've heard the giggles and moans coming from his turf house and

I've heard lots of stories—but *biting* ears and necks still seems strange to me.

However... it does FEEL good. Far, far better than I ever could have imagined.

"I am," he rumbles as his teeth find my shoulder, his voice rough, guttural, "marking you as a dragon marks his mate." He bites me again.

I cry out and my fingers spear into his hair, clutching him. *Why* does this feel good?

He folds himself over me and cups his hand under one of my breasts, holding it up like it's an offering.

"Nooo," I moan, experiencing too much and feeling too good to tense up. Despite the fact that a dragon is using me as his chew toy, I'm also aware of how surprisingly swollen I've become below. And, as my thighs slip past one another with startling ease, I find I've achieved a state of near-*saturation*. Who knew my cream would gather from dragon bites?

Halki's eyes gleam as he briefly makes eye contact—and then his focus is stolen by my nipple, and he pounces on it with his mouth.

He pulls it onto his tongue and sucks on it.

I've heard of this act—breast play, of course I have—but I had no context as to how incredible it feels to have a man's mouth latched on to such a sensitive area. With each tug from his mouth, I feel a spark race to the apex of my thighs, causing heat to flare in my stomach. "Halki!" I gasp.

He bites my nipple.

I shriek and clutch at the back of his neck. But for having sharp teeth, he's unbelievably... *gentle* somehow. Because it doesn't *hurt* like a true bite, and when I regain the use of my muscles enough to lift my head and glance down at myself, I'm not bleeding anywhere.

Halki transfers his attention to my other breast, and I brace myself when he closes his mouth over my nipple here too...

But he only draws at it with his tongue, adding a sucking pressure before he pulls away.

My body sags a little in a strange sort of disappointment.

A laugh rasps out from between my dragon's bright white teeth, making my eyes shoot to his.

He drags his cheek over my shoulder before sinking to the level of my breast again, and after rasping his scaly face there, he strikes with his mouth.

The flash of pain is chased by a burst of pleasure that hits me square between the legs even harder than before. "Why do I want this? Why does this feel good?" I ask, dazed.

"Because I'm a Crested Merlin, and we're amazing at everything we do," Halki replies. He sounds entirely serious.

I blink at the top of his head. "Um, just so you know, humility may not be one of your strong suits."

"Eh. That's a well-known fact among dragonkind." His hands skate down my sides and grip my hips, hard. He runs his tongue down the line of my stomach, making all of my skin jump, making my cheeks flush hot, stopping just above my curly mound. He looks up at me and grins. "But who needs to be humble when I'm magnificent?"

And then his thick fingers expertly part my lower lips and his knuckles drag past my swollen center of pleasure.

"NGNHA!" is what I shout.

Halki purrs loudly and teases along my insides with his fingers, stretching me, testing, seeking something. "I wonder," he manages to speak through the rattling noise his chest and throat are emitting, his lids low in a way that's making my heart race, "if you are like they say dragon females are, and you have a special sweet spot tucked inside your vent."

Vent? I shake my head to clear the image of a snake with its tail popped back, its hatch open—the one that expels and takes in breeding stuff as well as voids chalky waste. *Gross.* I shake my head harder.

Halki's eyes meet mine, and for a moment he looks crestfallen. If he were in his dragon form, this might be a literal happening with his real frill deflating at my answer.

"Not you," I tell him. "I was picturing a snake's—never mind. Yes, I have a sweet spot, and if you keep doing what you're doing, you're going to find it."

Halki rises over me, his breath fanning along my cheek before he drops his chin and drags his tongue up my throat, clearly pleased with this news.

His fingers keep circling inside me, slow and blindly, pleasurable but just off center from where my body would be best served by his attention.

"Pretend you're aiming for my belly button," I pant, feeling wetness at the side of my mouth. Oh my Venys, am I drooling? Swiping at my face with the back of my wrist, I return my hand to his shoulder where I had it perched, kneading and digging into his muscle with my nails.

"Your what?" he asks.

It takes me a moment to understand what he's asking.

My belly button. He doesn't have one; he doesn't know what one is.

With a clumsy hand, I shove between us and tap the depression on my stomach.

"Hm, I wondered what this belly divot was," he murmurs. "I'll ask you more about it later. For now..." his finger skates along the front of my vaginal wall with patience and curiosity. He whispers a touch over an area that makes my body lock up like I'm being hit with lightning.

"I am so pleased: I believe I've found it for you," he breathes—and his rumbly purr intensifies as he continues to coax more shaking, sweating, twitching tremors out of my thrilled system, making me cum for him—and he doesn't stop when he breaks my body for the first time. He keeps stroking the magic spot he's found, like it'll give him extra treasure if he turns it inside out and shakes the hell out of it.

He's nearly doing just that.

He uses two fingers to tap the sensitized area, making me muffle a scream as I quake from my womb to my *toes*. Pressure builds and builds and builds—until I feel liquid pulse out of me in time to my convulsing.

Instantly, I slam my thighs together, mortified. "It's not urine," I tell him quickly. "I've heard of this. It's—"

"I know," Halki says, and from the sizzling satisfaction in his eyes as he proudly draws out his fingers and begins to lick them clean, I realize he's not put off by my involuntary squirt of excitement at all. In fact, he's clearly proud and pleased.

It's strangely thrilling.

My inhibitions shrink even more.

He shifts, and his staff spills a trail of hot greasy fluid across my thigh. I tense, thinking that he's gotten so excited after pleasuring me that he's spontaneously cum and this will be an end to our session as I've often heard the horrified complaint from my tribesisters *('Those are wasted babies that were just spilled!')*. But Halki shifts again, gently humping me, and his cock continues to profusely leak—and he's completely unworried. The edginess and need in his eyes is not the look of a man who is satisfied yet, and if he's cumming, he isn't doing it in spurts; he's oozing. When I reach between us and brush at it, the fluid is slick and thickens against my finger like jam, sticky and—when I dare to bring it to my mouth—I find it sweet.

"Blazing fires," Halki chokes.

My gaze flies to his.

His eyes are wide as he stares at me. "You are the most seductive female."

My cheeks heat, and it's a struggle not to duck or avert my gaze, but I'm flattered at his praise, especially when I was only curious, not striving to be seductive. There's something incredibly powerful about being seen as desirable, especially when I'm only being myself.

I dig my shoulders deeper into the bedding, his castings nudging me as I do, and bring my knees up to Halki's sides. I slide my calves over his back and cross my ankles, locking him to me. Inadvertently, I moan as his shaft fits along my slit, his hot oil mixing with my cream.

Halki hisses and grips himself, fisting his staff at the root. His eyes glitter as he gazes down my body and fixes his eyes on his obscene organ as it thumps against my swollen lips.

He growls.

His thumb finds my clit, and then he leans back enough for his cock to pop up between us, glossy with my wetness and his strange emissions. He prods the head of it at the top of my sex, making me twitch and suck in a breath.

The contact feels nice. And then his feathery accessories wrap around my clit and start tickling it.

Maybe it's the added stimulation of seeing Halki's hungry eyes locked on me as he touches me this time, but I screech in languages I don't even recognize. The little moth-penis-feathers are merciless as they draw out the most intense series of orgasms I've ever experienced. *He could have started with this.* Or maybe not. I was nervous about this part of him touching me, and he probably didn't miss that fact.

If it matters, I'm reticent about his accoutrements no longer. My limbs are flailing, my neck is arched back, my mouth is open—I don't even care that I've partially fallen against one of Halki's castings. I even know which one, because dimly, I'm aware of the cool smoothness of the bull's ring as it steals warmth from my skin.

I'm stammering prayers mingled with effusive statements of gratitude when Halki draws the feathery parts away with clear reluctance.

Gasping, shaking—bleary-eyed and blissful—I try to focus on Halki's face. My hands ineffectually pet along his arms as he sits up on his heels, angles the head of his staff down, and slides into me with a deep, seemingly endless thrust.

And although he coaxed my body to admit him, I still wasn't prepared for how it would *feel* to be stuffed full of Halki's organ earlier. Unbelievably, it feels even bigger than it looks. My breathing is affected as he drives in, separating my insides.

At once, I'm excited as well as feeling overpowered by the sheer thickness and iron-hardness of him.

And then he begins to draw himself out. The slide is slow, long, and feels so good it hurts. I gasp his name as my insides begin to flutter through his retreat.

Something snaps in my dragon. He plunges inside me with a rough thrust that makes his sack slap below the sensitive, stretched place where I'm joined to him.

I cry out, and he clutches me and rides me harder. His pupils have spread until there's almost no evergreen iris to be seen. It makes him look crazed. To complete the impression, his lips are slightly parted, his sharp teeth bared.

The illicit tempo of his stones spanking my ass intensifies. It's wild. It's primal. I love it, love everything about this—his weight, I love the smell of him, I love the way he handles me, with frenzied reverence. With burning need.

He's breathing raggedly, his special oil glands along the sides of his member more evident than ever as streams of unguent wetness exit with every rapid withdraw of his hips, the overfilled spills running down my crack as he crams himself inside me again.

And *again*.

Hands slide to my hips where fingers dig into my flesh, his dragon-man's nails pricking me in ten buzzing places—and Halki gives a grunting, powerful thrust, grinding us together.

I bite my lip, moaning.

He nuzzles my cheek with his nose, hips slowly parting from mine.

I sigh and relax, sinking into the decadence of the physical stimulation.

Without warning, he bangs himself back inside me and explodes.

I cry out at the sensation of intensely hot dragon sackjuice spraying forcefully against my walls.

Halki bites my shoulder, his teeth sinking deep.

He keeps me pinned underneath of him in all ways—by his heavy body, his piercing rod, and now his fangs.

Spray upon spray of semen fills me up, hitting my insides in pulses, setting off strange pleasure quakes low in my belly.

His special penis antennae pet me softly, a sharp contrast to his claiming holds on me everywhere else.

After a lifetime, he withdraws his teeth and laps lazily at my shoulder like he's a lion of the mountains, cleaning his well-used mate.

It feels weirdly good.

He sighs atop me, relaxing. I squish under him, absorbing his weight with a satisfaction I never knew was possible.

We lay this way, panting—and yes, with me slowly suffocating.

I should tell him to move, but I can't drum up the wherewithal to care. If I die like this, it will have been worth it. And now I get it, what Yatanak's always said about the sacrifice of dying during lusty sex being a price he feels like paying. *I get it now.*

A rattle starts up behind Halki's sternum; his purr shakes right into me, the vibrations only loosening my bones even more.

My hands play along the muscles of his sides, my fingers falling in the trenches carved between his sawing ribs, digging in when he inhales, enjoying the way he exhales a shuddery breath.

When I drag my nails up towards his shoulders, Halki groans and drops even heavier atop me, burying his face in my throat. It's an oddly vulnerable gesture; there's a tug on my heart as my whole body fills with warmth just to have him resting on me like this.

After a moment, he falls off of me and rolls to his back, dragging me on top of him.

Our hearts pound against each other, gradually calming as they sync beats. And all the while, Halki's gaze stays glued to mine, his hands caressing me tenderly. Soon, they touch me possessively. And when he's urging me to position myself so that I'm skewered astride him, he's baring his teeth, and his oil-glazed staff is sliding into my thoroughly shocked slit.

To think that it started the morning a virgin, for all intents and purposes. It's had quite the awakening.

...More like *attacking*.

His eyes capturing mine, I'm sure he can see my shock. "Again?" I croak. "Really?"

When he smiles, Halki's teeth glint. "Welcome to mate fever."

CHAPTER 20

Nalle

WHEN THE SUN DOMINATES the sky and 'the lusty taskmaster of a moon is gone,' as Halki puts it, we emerge from our lodgehouse. It's only been a night's worth of heat, but Halki looks thinner, and I'm a cum-filled, sticky-swollen mess when I greet my tribe. Halki's gripping my hand less like he's holding it and more like he's shackling it to keep me from getting away.

Like I could. I'm walking bow-legged, my hip is complaining just enough to give me a proud little thrill—and when we round the curve of the path and everyone comes into view, my entire tribe gapes at us, all of them at their fires with their morning tea.

Then they break out in applause.

What follows is a gauntlet of good-natured snickers and ribbing and ribald comments that nearly make my dragon blush as we wind our way to the latrine and a morning bath.

We're only slightly waylaid when Kulla shouts that she'll trade me a skein of Qiviut yarn for a ride on Halki.

Qiviut yarn?

I stutter to a halt. I throw my head back and order Halki, "You'll only have to do this one time." My eyes widen as I rub my hands together with glee. "Unless she offers me another skein."

I'm mostly teasing.

Mostly.

Halki snorts smoke at my face, bends at his knees, and plants his shoulder into my solar plexus, tossing me up and over himself until my view is his back and his fine ass. "You don't get to trade me for *yarn,* female."

Secretly, I'm pleased he wants no one but me. Still, I pretend to fight about this, shaking my head at him even though he can't see me. "You don't know how amazing this stuff is, Halki!"

"More amazing than a Great Crested Merlin?" he asks, sounding disbelieving. "More amazing than *me?*"

And he has every right to question the notion. As I stare down the meaty, muscled expanse of his powerful back and proud haunches, I know I will never want to give this up.

I sigh happily. But I inject regret into my tone like I'm conceding valuable, rare things. Like Qiviut. "Okay." I lightly fondle the part of his butt that isn't covered by the loincloth. "Only if she offers me three skeins."

He brings his palm to my butt. I jump, expecting him to spank his handful, but he doesn't. He just cups me. It feels... too nice for public. At least my dress is long enough that I look as decent and dignified as one can in this position—you know, being shouldered by a dragon who doesn't want to be studded out for yarn.

"What *is* Qiviut yarn?" he asks.

I exhale a dreamy sigh. "Only the most sumptuous of wools. Halki, it's so soft, you'll be amazed when you feel it." I slap at the hands of my tribesisters who are trying to touch Halki's barely-covered rump as he parts the crowd. "Mine!" I snarl at them, making Halki rumble in approval.

Kulla waves her skein of Qiviut as we pass her, hoping to tempt us. It's nearly working for one of us.

"Is it softer than the center of you?" Halki asks, distracting me as I reach out for it.

I pause, trying to twist around him to see his face, but I can't. He adjusts his hold on my thighs, his hand warm, his scales rough on my skin where my dress doesn't reach. "You mean my heart?"

"No." His hand that he has over my hind end slides down until he's cupping me in front of everyone, making me yelp and shove my palms into his back, bracketing his spine, trying to rear up on him. "This," he says. "This part of you right here." He squeezes.

I throw my hand over my mouth to stifle the embarrassing moan I make in reaction.

He shoves up my dress. He ignores my shout. "I don't think anything is softer than your center," Halki informs me, sharing his opinion so innocently that it feels extra lubricious as he shoves his finger between my thighs and dips inside me.

My tribesisters kindly disappear as my dragonman violates me all the way to the latrine, then the bathhouse where he takes me hard enough to make me scream—and no one interrupts us to make further offers.

This might have something to do with Halki's bone-shivering growl of, "And you would trade *this*—"

(The bathhouse shakes on its foundation from the force of his thrust—and my moan is loud and tortured and filthy.)

"—for mere *yarn?*"

(Clearly, my dragon has never touched wool like Qiviut. But he's made his point. Even for Qiviut, he's convinced me not to trade him.)

...Not that I really would have. And about halfway through a punishing thrust that makes me nearly sing for him, I assure him of that fact.

His answering grin tells me that he knew I was only goading him all along.

He ruts me until I can barely remember my name. His though, I never lose the capability to moan.

When I'm dressed (and Halki is more or less dressed in his loin-cloth), we exit the bathhouse and make our way to the center of our village, where everyone is going about daily chores. Chores I've neglected. I look around with concern. "How's our bum lamb doing?"

Fenna huffs. "What do you mean *your* lamb? Every feeding that little thing expands more and more. Soon it'll be a fat, spoiled ball of wool."

"Good!" I say, relieved.

"Is the orphan's dam still producing milk?" Halki asks hopefully.

He hasn't been able to stop talking about it. Well, that's not quite true. It'd be more accurate to say that when he isn't pinning me down and driving into me hard enough to make me go blind, and when he isn't dragging me on top of him and urging me to ride him faster, *then* he's talking about food.

Breeding and food. They seem to be the main drives of a dragon.

Of course, eating and sex aren't mutually exclusive. I learned that lesson well and thoroughly.

A dreamy sigh catches in my throat when Halki glances at me sharply, his eyes hotter than a moment ago. It's as if he can read the turn my thoughts took.

"Here, dragon," Fenna says, marching to us and shoving an earthen-ware pitcher into his hands. "Sheep's milk. Still warm."

Halki carefully uses his clawed, mostly-human fingers to lift the clay lid and peer inside. "Oooh, thank you," he murmurs. And then he brings the pitcher lip up to his mouth and tips it back like it's sweet mead, not milk.

When he runs his tongue as far as it will reach inside of the up-turned, emptied pitcher, Fenna grimaces. "That was my pottery, but you can keep it."

Halki makes an appreciative noise, and fits the lid back onto the pitcher before running his tongue over his upper lip to clean away his milk mustache. "You are very kind."

Fenna sniffs and eyes the pitcher he tongued. "Yeah. You dragons bring out the 'kind' in me a lot lately." She's grumbling by the end of her statement, and then she whirls around and stalks off.

Wincing, I call after her, "Thank you for taking care of the lamb!"

"Whatever!" she calls back.

"We'll owe you!" I shout.

"She can have the next bachelor dragon we come upon," Halki offers. He glances at me and points to the pitcher held by the handle in his other hand. "I feel wretched for not thinking of you first. Did you want some?"

I bite back my smile. "A little late to ask." When he begins to look ashamed, I pat his scaly, broad shoulder. "It's all right, I'm only teasing. I've grown up with a lifetime of sheep's milk. I'm glad you enjoy it." I glance around us, chewing on my lip. "Where are your brothers?" I ask him out of the corner of my mouth.

Halki surveys our tribe with a superior air. "You're missing two clan sisters." Then he grins. "They must have mated them."

"Whaaat," I say, bug-eyed—because I didn't even notice I was missing tribeswomen. I have to scan over everyone again to see which two are gone.

Sassnitz is nowhere to be seen... and neither is Västra *or* Ingrid the goose. Oh no...

"I'm going to hunt," Halki announces. "A Crested Merlin can go the full length of a heat without eating, but I'd prefer to hunt during these times when I don't feel nearly as mating-maddened. Currently, I'm sated."

I snort. "You should be, you beast."

He growls smugly to that and snaps his teeth, making my skin shiver—and not because I'm scared. He squeezes my hand and gives me a bright smile. He also hands me his prized pitcher for safekeeping. "Another casting will be joining our collection. We'll have to arrange them with care. Last night, you were so overcome with fever that you managed to push the ones we have off of the bench."

"I remember," I murmur. I remember being 'overcome' several times, in fact, but then Halki would *stop* the activity to retrieve them and set them beside us again.

As far as I'm concerned, I'm a champion at biting my tongue when it comes to my mate's attraction to dried vomit.

"Happy hunting," I tell my dragon, tugging him down to me for a farewell kiss.

Kissing is something we haven't really done. Halki prefers nibbling, nuzzling, and biting whenever his mouth gets close.

But without sex clouding his thoughts, I'm able to get a quick peck to his surprised lips.

When I pull back enough to refocus, my throat closes up so fast I squeak.

Because Halki's eyes have gone full black.

I push away from him. "Oh, you animal! Behave yourself and go get your hunting done. A minute ago, you were excited to make yourself another casting, remember?"

He doesn't answer. He does begin to purr, though. And instead of turning into a dragon and flying off to hunt his next meal, he steps into me, his penetrating gaze setting fire to my insides.

He backs me up with his next step. And his next.

He's *stalking* me.

I don't even have time to decide if I should try to escape him or not. With a growl, he catches me up and throws me over his shoulder, dragging me back to the lodgehouse for more vigorous fucking.

EPILOGUE

HALKI

CRESTED MERLINS REFER to a group of dragons as a 'valor.'

Lacewing dragons refer to their groups as a 'court.'

Whatever collective term you prefer, during the blessedly long days before the blood moon takes over the sky (where we catch some respite from the nighttime mating heat), I catch Nalle all but one of my brothers, and nearly a dozen Lacewings. (As well as a Western Hydra that it took a great deal of skill to capture, considering it had nine simultaneous firepoints, but Nalle insisted I turn him loose because she feared he'd turn into a multi-headed man upon bonding, and she said the very idea 'creeped' her out.)

Not that it should have mattered since he'd be bonding to a woman other than my Nalle, but she was adamant, thus I let him go.

As far as the Lacewings though, those we kept. And because Nalle once promised a favor to the Middle Plains Tribe, that's where we take the latest mate-fevered bunch of bachelors. They're so crazed to breed they don't ask what *kind* of females we're taking them to. Although they're in such a bad way, we don't think the idea of humans will make them hesitate.

Making good on her vow turns out to be quite the reward for Nalle; rather than delivering the Lacewings and immediately leaving, the Middle Plains residents insist that Nalle accept trades for the dragons we've brought them as the males bond to women and begin turning into mating-crazed men.

We settle on trading for weaving threads in colors that will please Nalle. The Middle Plains Tribe are experts at the application of dyes and pigments on wools and skins, and with extensive flocks of interesting creatures *(llamas,* Nalle calls them—and I'm curious as to what llamas might taste like, but Nalle tells me it would be frowned-upon if I consumed any), the tribe has much to offer that Nalle has never before seen.

I learned she favors the color amethyst. She blushed when she admitted this preference. An odd reaction, I thought—until her eyes met mine and I had a flash of memory where I marked her back with my cum—my amethyst-colored cum.

This revelation made me grin.

I'd vowed to gift Nalle with amethyst-dyed everything from now on.

When we return to our own clan, Nalle and I are deep in discussions of what our blended offspring might be like.

"No matter what," I promise her as I set her down onto her feet, "I, as your capable Crested Merlin, will of course take part in all aspects of rearing our young just as you do."

Nalle pats my foreleg. "There are a *few* things you can't do."

I tilt my head, eyeing her. "Name them."

"You can't give birth."

My tail flips before twitching to the other side. "Well, I've been releasing thousands upon thousands of sperm. It is perhaps a form of birthing."

Nalle stops walking and gives me a disturbing stare. "When I deliver, you'd better hope I forget this conversation. And I suggest you don't mention it again."

Strange female. "All right." I shuffle my wings. "What's the next dissimilarity?"

She bends her knees and tips herself until she's nearly turned herself upside down while standing up. Her head is completely angled so that she's viewing my undercarriage. "You don't have nipples. So milk production is out too."

"Not true," I tell her proudly.

She straightens and eyes me in wide-eyed shock. "You have nipples? That *work?*"

I puff smoke as I chuckle. "That would just be strange. No, Crested Merlins secrete crop milk for our young."

Nalle stops walking again. "What now?"

I point to my neck. "See this? This is my crop. When our clutch hatches, I'll be lactating by secreting a yellow semi-solid substance high in fats and proteins and beneficial bacteria."

Nalle blinks up at me rapidly. "Where does it come from?"

"From here," I repeat, tapping my crop.

"No, I mean what—where does the secretion even come from up in there? Are you eating some sort of special liquid or—"

"My regular diet will suffice. I'll simply need to ingest a larger quantity of food."

"Good God."

I tilt my head at her, but continue. "As for where the milk comes from, my crop lining will detach in small stages and emulsify. I'll regurgitate it for our offspring until they're ready to leave the nest."

Nalle covers her mouth with her hand.

I nudge her with my snout. "Oooh, *drhema,* stay here. I smell antelope! They're fast becoming my favorite meal to hunt. Not to mention we'll secure another tawny-colored casting for our collection. I'm rather fond of how many we have in that shade."

Nalle covers her eyes with her other hand. Muffled, I hear her mutter, "*Yay.*"

I bound through the grass towards the herd, feeling light and happy and joyful, just as my mate surely does.

~Nalle~

"UGGGGH," I MOAN INTO my hands as I drag my feet back into the village proper.

"What's wrong with you?" Västra asks, carrying Ingrid the goose. It's only a little surprising to see her holding her own goose. Västra's dragon (Danelagh) usually appoints himself the duty of goose-keeper, tending to the bird as if it's their feathered child.

And since she's here, I decide that because she's mated to Halki's brother, she might want to know what I just learned. "Did you know that dragons produce milk?"

Västra frowns, looking curious rather than disbelieving. "How?" Something occurs to her, and her brows go up and her lips tug up in a smile. "Wait, are they like pigeons?"

"Are they like *pigeons?*" I stare at her. "They're dragons."

She spins her forefinger, rotating her whole wrist. "Right, right—but they regurgitate the 'milk,' don't they?"

My jaw drops. "You scare me sometimes. I don't even want to know how you know this."

She rolls her eyes. "Haven't you ever watched pigeons feed their squabs?"

"I can't say that I've paid attention. Silly me, I never thought that the mysteries of pigeon-feeding would relate to anything in my life."

"Weren't you wrong."

"Apparently. Okay, I'm going to find someone else to share this news with. Someone who will be properly horrified with me."

Västra smirks. "You think it'll matter to any of us?"

I pretend to sigh in defeat—but I'm smiling. Because we *are* happy After Tamworth and Danelagh found mates among my tribesisters and were pleased with the development, they hunted down more bachelor dragons until there wasn't one unmated woman in our tribe.

Now, thanks to Halki, Danelagh, and Tamworth, we're branching out to neighboring tribes too. If we hurry, we could help pair loads of dragons who are miserable with mate heat to human women who would love a devoted, protective, virile man. (One with a few eccentricities, but hey, dragon mates are never boring.)

"Nalle, I have returned!" my never-boring mate announces as he smoothly lands beside me and Västra.

I lean against his foreleg and I'm not ashamed of how I stare up at him adoringly. So he's eccentric. He's also pretty wonderful. "Did you enjoy your antelope?"

"Immensely. Thank you for inquiring."

"Did you get to add another special yellow casting to the collection?"

Halki looks pleased that I asked, and sits down on his haunches. "I'll be adding it shortly." His abdomen spasms a little, the first sign that he's about to hork up his regurgitated brick.

"Great." I send a look over my shoulder to Västra, who grins and struts away probably to reunite with her own dragon. Ingrid follows her, honking.

A disturbing, disturbing retching sound commences from my mate, but I'm barely fazed. Not anymore.

And just think: after a few weeks of Halki producing 'milk' for our children, I might not be grossed out by that either.

I shudder and decide that the line will be drawn somewhere.

Halki proudly raises his latest casting. "Just look at this one, Nalle! It has pronghorns sticking out of it."

"Ouch," I say, wincing for him. "Bet that felt great coming up."

"It did not. But it will be lovely for the collection."

I make a noise that I halfway hope is agreeable.

"We're going to require a lodgehouse expansion," Halki informs me as we turn and begin trekking to ours so that he can put his casting away.

"For the babies we'll raise?" I ask hopefully.

"For them too," my dragon says with a nod. "But also because a dragon produces well over three hundred castings per solar."

If I had a wall handy, I'd beat my head against it. We pass by Yatanak, who has been relieved not to bear the burden of servicing our whole tribe anymore. He's even settled down with one woman. He raises a hand in a wave when he sees me and Halki pass by.

I wave back, remembering his advice that essentially landed us all here. Without a word exchanged between us, I shake my head at him, and he laughs, rightly guessing what I'm thinking about. Shortly after Halki's mating fever began, during one of the daytime-periods where his heat wasn't making him starved for me and completely mating-crazy, I made sure to have a word with Yatanak about 'knee-high' dragons and sending me off with a damned fishing hook to catch one.

Yatanak stunned me by sharing that he assumed dragons were knee-high because that was the size of the dragon that used to stalk me.

"You *knew* Halki used to stalk me? Why didn't you TELL me?!" I'd gasp-asked.

Yatanak said he nearly shouted the plains down in warning when he saw what I'd attracted. But before he could holler my name, something stopped him. It was something about the way the dragon watched me. Not predatory. *Proprietary.*

That night, Yatanak told our tribe what he found. They were undecided on how to proceed—should they try to catch the dragon, or kill him?—but their plans turned out to be moot anyway.

No dragon would be shadowing me any longer because unbeknownst to us, Halki had been caught by his parents.

As I was digesting this news, old Yatanak smugly pointed out that hooking my dragon *worked.*

I smirk to myself, and send a look up at Halki that makes his eyes turn darker. And on the end of his snout, one of his nostril shields still has a tiny hook-sized hole in it from where I caught him.

Oh yes, it worked. Better than I could have ever imagined. Rather than training him to fight other tribes, he's helped us *and* them in a way that's repaired past trespasses. He's even flown me to visit my brother (who insists that his women will have no dragons; he's enough for all of them—blech!) and gifted him with dragon gold (melted down bull nose rings) as a 'bride price' for me, something that made my brother smirk about to no end.

Luckily for both males, I thought it was a pretty cute gesture. I was touched. It further solidified for me that Halki is amazing. He's made me happier than I could have dreamed. My dragon is perfect.

"Would you like the honor of arranging this casting?" Halki asks earnestly. We've reached our lodgehouse.

All right. *Close* to perfect. I clear my throat and tilt my head back, pursing my lips at my dragon, bemused. "I'm good."

"Are you certain?"

"Oh yeah. Thanks for offering me the honor though."

Halki's tail winds around me and he tugs me to the side of his face, his horn base clunking against my shoulder. "Of course, *drhema*. I adore you."

I wrap my arms around his long, scaly face. "That's always good to hear, my wonderful—" *weird, vomiting, oddly-sweet* "—other half. I love you, Halki."

He purrs as he changes into a man and hauls me inside our lodgehouse. (With his casting, of course.)

He hands it off to me to hold so he can properly manhandle me towards the bedding benches. We don't reach it though; he doesn't even care when I drop the casting in favor of bracing myself as he ruts me damn near through the lodge wall.

Happy sigh.

As I said, my dragon is perfect.

THE END

AUTHOR NOTE

DID YOU HAVE FUN? =D Want to read the story of one of Halki's other brothers?

If so, check out *The Mermaid and the Dragon:* https://amzn.to/3dzDUyW

If you're wondering when the next *Stolen by an Alien* book will arrive, the answer is **Soon,** yay! I got the edits back on Bash's 1st draft back in February (Bash is the grumpy Rakhii introduced at the end of *Craved by an Alien)* and the 2nd draft is nearly done. Just a couple more passes and this puppy will be good to go! =D

For now, if you'd like to read more dragon stories set in the same world that Halki & Nalle live in, the following books are up for grabs in any order, and are complete standalones.

To Touch a Dragon by Naomi Lucas: https://amzn.to/2MwG1Yr

To Tame a Dragon by Tiffany Roberts: https://amzn.to/2Y3kc8m

To Seduce a Dragon by Poppy Rhys: https://amzn.to/2Y3C17h

:) I hope Halki and Nalle's story made you smile and happy-sigh! <3 If you get a chance to leave a review, you know what this does for an author like me. ***THANK YOU.*** And thank you for grabbing this book! I really hope you enjoyed!!

Sincerest Squeeze-hugs!

Amanda ♥

Trivia Fun!

Gooses

SEBASTOPOL GEESE REALLY do have curly feathers. In fact, in Germany they are called *Lockengans* which means "curl-goose." Of all the geese varieties we had, Sebbies were the nicest and least likely to harass the dogs. Or chase people. Or beat children. Ahhhh, geese! So many fond memories! ;D

Sring not String

Nalle mentions trading for a *sring* flute. The sring is a real-life musical instrument; it's a flute used by shepherds in Armenia.

Yarn Lovers Understand

Qiviut yarn is a real thing. It's collected from Arctic Musk Ox and it's quite rare—and quite expensive. But the *most* expensive yarn comes care of a wild animal called the vicuña. Apparently the wool collection is a trip. They round up wild herds, shear them, then turn them loose. Since they're related to llamas and I've sheared some unhappy *not* wild llamas, I do not envy the people who have this wool-rustling job.

Create-a-Dragon

I was so excited to design a dragon! =D I looked at raptors (the predatory bird-kind, not the dinosaur kind, although I love me some *Jurassic Park*) and frilled lizards from Australia. For the raptor research I settled mostly on Merlin falcons. And while regurgitated remains are referred to as pellets in the wide world of ornithology, Falconers call pellets castings. Falcons cast pellets like Merlin dragons do, but falcons do not produce milk for their chicks. That honor really does go to pigeons.

That was Real.

Pigeons, doves, flamingos—all of them really do burp up their throat lining for their kids. Nature is *fascinating*. (And apparently I'm a little milk-source intolerant; I don't blink at the notion of drinking milk out of a teat *(even a sheep's* ;)*)* but vomiting your digestive tract into your baby's mouth? NOPE. XD!)

Crack These Open to Cure Book Hangovers

NEED A COCKBOOK FOR your kitchen? Thanks to Dravon for sharing this! ;D *50 Ways to Eat Cock* https://amzn.to/3d2OduY

Haven't read this one yet, but it was recommended to me by a diehard KA fan and my Kindle was hungry: *Dream Maker* by Kristen Ashley https://amzn.to/3gQCthA

I like this author. This one was a good read if you're a fan of her books & style: *Third Life* by Noelle Adams https://amzn.to/3czhb4U

Hmmm, I'm told I won't get my romance fix here, but I'll have a thrilling time anyway. *The Spider Heist* by Jason Kasper https://amzn.to/3dCMehv

For a sci-fi romance adventure to balance out my ebook bag, I've got *Barbarian's Treasure* by Ruby Dixon loaded up and ready to enjoy! https://amzn.to/2Y2e0gU

Books & Audiobooks by Amanda...

ARE YOU WONDERING WHAT else I've written? BLESS YOU! I hope whatever you grab, that you have FUN ♥ *GIANT HUG*

Stolen by an Alien—Arokh and Angie's story ebook: https://amzn.to/2A6sH9T

This book is also available in Audio, narrated by the talented Nick Cracknell: https://adbl.co/2N7WXHF

Rescued by an Alien—Zadeon and Callie's story ebook: http://amzn.to/2EZEitg

Audiobook voiced by Nick Cracknell: https://adbl.co/2Nx8WxR

(WARNING: This one has some Dark times. This couple's love is beautiful though, and they get their Happily Ever After.)

Won by an Alien—Brax, Tara, and Tac'Mot's story is here: http://amzn.to/2FeuFGl

Audiobook narrated by Teddy Hamilton and Callie Dalton: https://amzn.to/2zUkHWu

(If you had to classify this one, it's *almost* Reverse Harem. This is an MFM book, which means there are two (alien) guys and one woman but it's not *quite* menage, because Brax is a Rakhii, and you know this means he doesn't share his female. Slight problem: his female is bonded to Tac'Mot.)

Craved by an Alien—Dohrein and Gracie's story: https://amzn.to/2Qn4lwo

Audiobook voiced by Nick Cracknell: https://adbl.co/2s6gN96

The Alien Nanny for Christmas—Mitteeku & Gwen's love story stands alone but has some cute Easter eggs for those who've followed the *Stolen* universe: https://amzn.to/3cMfEcu

Blind Fall, the standalone story that answers the question you've all been asking me: *"Is the guide dog okay?"*

Spoiler: She's MORE than okay. ♥ This is Breslin and Sanna's story. If you read this one, I hope you have fun.

https://amzn.to/2PvoaAm

Audiobook narrated by Teddy Hamilton and Callie Dalton: https://amzn.to/2WImX17

Beth's Stable, a reverse harem romance for movie-lovers. Just trust me. ;)

https://amzn.to/2ZFxyLx

A fun side project *Not* related to the *Stolen* series:

Valos of Sonhadra Series

Alluvial, Book 1: https://amzn.to/2OhfX33

Tempest, Book 2, written by Poppy Rhys: https://amzn.to/2uPfihv

Galvanizing Sol, Book 3, by Amanda Milo & Poppy Rhys: https://amzn.to/2AgxDZE

Another side project:

Contaminated, a Cosmic Fairy Tale https://amzn.to/36RFbhS

(Erreck and Nancy's story, which features Simmi as a lovably gruff secondary character.)

Contagion: Simmi's standalone, germphobic HEA story https://amzn.to/2ElEVuk

The Pet Project: https://amzn.to/2UAU3ff

The Pet Project: *Unnatural Selection* https://amzn.to/2URRAxl

The Pet Project: *JoAyyn* https://amzn.to/2ybVHfV

DragonTribe Books:

To Desire a Dragon (a.k.a. DRAGON HOOKER): https://amzn.to/36opdMx

To Enchant a Dragon (a.k.a. MERMAID AND THE DRAG-ON): https://amzn.to/3dzDUyW

And a random coloring book that I drew for fun :D https://amzn.to/2MSk3Pu

About the Author

AMANDA MILO IS A COLLECTOR of the randomest trivia. *Did you know that Kiwi fruit plants have separate genders? You need both in order to make Kiwi fruits happen. Isn't that cool??*

She's concerned about river otter bite pressure—she hasn't had a chance to test this out, but frankly, this is the part that's holding her back from appropriating and testing the relocation (aka wildlife theft) of a small family of adorable river otters.

...To the bathtub. (They're basically like slick-furred rubber duckies, but with lots of teeth, right? Right.)

Extended contemplation of this plan has led to the permission to adopt more ferrets, which makes her very happy. So does her extensive, wacky-patterned, thigh-high sock collection—though ferrets, it must be noted, do not play well with pretty socks. The crazy, clawed thieves!

She invites you to hang out with her in the *Amanda Milo's Minions* Facebook group. (She didn't name the group! XD Readers have great senses of humor!)

Thank you for picking up this book. Amanda hopes that you had a lovely time. ♥

Printed in Great Britain
by Amazon

43391256R00087